VIVA KNIEVEL!

A Novel By
JOHN STANLEY

Based on a screenplay by Antonio Santillan
and Norman Katkov
Story by Antonio Santillan

AVON
PUBLISHERS OF BARD, CAMELOT AND DISCUS BOOKS

VIVA KNIEVEL is an original publication of Avon Books. This work has never before appeared in book form.

Photos courtesy of Warner Bros., Inc., and Metropolitan Theatres Corp.

AVON BOOKS
A division of
The Hearst Corporation
959 Eighth Avenue
New York, New York 10019

First Avon Printing, June, 1977

HELLCAT ON WHEELS

Knievel climbed the ramp at eighty-five miles an hour, leaning into the onrush of air that seemed to enfold and engulf him.

He floated.

He felt the thrust of the engine, the surge of the machine.

He was an eagle. Free from the world which had spawned him, from the spectators who had made him rich, from the dumb brutish driving fearless force that had made him a defier of everything mortal man feared.

Then came harmony.

Evel Knievel and the orange machine were as one. Flesh metamorphosed into chrome-plated steel; the throbbing motor pistons transmuted into blood-pumping valves. It was a union born of love and need—man's love for machine, the machine's need for man to give it purpose and effect and direction.

It was almost a perfect union.

Almost.

1

King of the Jumpers

THEY swarmed by the thousands into Wembley Stadium, where England's finest rugby players had upheld the honor of the empire since the vast amphitheater arena had been constructed for the British Exhibition in 1924–25.

They motored from as far away as Liverpool to the north and Plymouth to the west to see him perform his act of derring-do. Some described it as an act of insanity.

They were little different from their counterparts in America—they were average people looking for a thrill; an extra dash of excitement which the twentieth century didn't always offer in its day-to-day mundaneness. They came to see an adventurer and an explorer and a defier.

Most of those who made the sojourn bore no malice: they were concerned for his safety and hoped nothing would go wrong. A few even prayed for his well-being.

There were always a handful among the thousands who felt differently. These were the sadists who wanted only to see him spatter his brains, or spill his blood, over the turf.

The gladiatorial arena was not entirely a thing of the past—not yet.

This handful of unsavory and undesirable individuals came for blood and they cried out for blood.

Robert Craig "Evel" Knievel was in no hurry to give it.

A man who defies death can never be in a hurry. In fact, it was part of Knievel's showmanship to keep the packed grandstands waiting before a performance. Not only did this give the concessionaires additional time to sell their food, drink and souvenirs, but it built tension, made people fidgety and nervous. Fidgety and nervous people talked. They spoke with impatience, doubt, deep-rooted respect and loyalty. These fidgety and nervous people became a chorus that sang a paean to his bravura. Or a dirge to his insanity.

"Time to get off the pot, Knievel."

"The hotshot American must've lost his nerve."

"Blimey, I do think the bloody bloke has turned tail."

"Five bob says he shows and he jumps."

"That's a bet you'll have to back up with more than your mouth, chum."

"These Americans, I say, they live on nothing but publicity. Whole country's built on it."

"Hot air, that's all that keeps the likes of Knievel buoyant."

"Ten minutes late already, he is."

"I can see him now, chaps, running through Piccadilly Circus with his tail between his legs."

"He chickened at Snake River, he did."

"Manure-on-Manchester. The system malfunctioned."

"Aborted . . . that's what they call it in America."

"He'll never show. A pound he never shows."

"I'll take that bet, I will, just to close your bloomin' foul mouth."

"He'll show. And run that Harley of his straight across the backsides of the lot of you."

Knievel listened and smiled. Those were the voices he wanted to hear. *I don't care what you say about me, just say it.*

Knievel returned to the pit to join Will Atkins, a brooding figure of a man clad in orange coveralls. His face was craggy and pocked, like the terrain of a cross-country motorbike endurance course. Tiny trails of perspiration were testament to his diligence as a mechanic. His face was unshaven, his eyes bloodshot, his grayish hair receding, his cheeks ravaged by the effects of too much drinking. The once-granite jaw was now a parody of flab. Will was leaner and taller than Knievel, and at the age of fifty looked closer to sixty. Life with the hard-living, hard-pushing Knievel and hours spent hovering above a bottle of bourbon had taken their toll.

Knievel noticed lubricant stains crisscrossing Will's face in silly patterns and he commented on them but drew no response. Will was a private person; too damned private for his own good. Solemn, taciturn, withdrawn . . . not so good when you were surrounded by thrill-happy crowds every day who wanted only to see a splash of showmanship.

But Knievel could overlook that—Will was his closest friend and functioned superbly as a mechanic, checking the

6

bikes and making certain the equipment on the field was properly positioned before each jump.

Atkins possessed a fierce, dedicated loyalty Knievel found to be an uncommon trait among the men he knew, but it was well concealed behind Will's gruffness and his seeming inarticulateness. He would be the last to express his true feelings.

"Crowd's starting to get a little restless," said Will, twisting the handlebars of a jet-fire orange Harley-Davidson XR 750, checking for smoothness in turning. "I'm tightening the steering damper knob. It'll keep the cycle straighter."

"That's great for when I'm up in the air flying," replied Knievel, "not so great on the floor."

"Just keep that in mind when you're performing the wheelies. God, it's hot," said Will, wiping his forehead.

"That's good. Let them sweat a little. Gets the adrenalin worked up."

Will made an adjustment, turning the tiny screwdriver with the precision of a doctor wielding a scalpel during a life-or-death operation.

Will stood back.

The Machine was ready and waiting.

It was peculiar how the Harley always took on a personality of her own a few minutes before a big jump. As though she too were defying him to climb aboard—a challenge to see if he had the dexterity and the coolness and the coordination to keep her aloft, on a smooth course, arcing gracefully.

The Machine gleamed and waited. Knievel never tired of scanning her before each jump: 750 c.c. O.H.V. engine with tuned exhaust pipes and a 748 c.c. overhead valve; Tillotson racing carburetor with standard ratio; four-speed transmission and aluminum pushrods; a welded high body tube frame with swing arm rear suspension; lightweight fiberglass seat-fender with foam cushion; a fiberglass gas tank with two-and-one-half-gallon capacity for ethyl (always ethyl goddam it and don't let anyone catch you pumping anything but); Ceriani racing front fork with aluminum fork bracket; Girling racing rear shock absorbers; nineteen-inch aluminum wheels and rims; front tire a 4.00 × 19 Pirelli Universal; rear tire a 4.00 × 19 Goodyear All-Traction.

She was a beautiful machine but she was more than that.

She was a Flying Machine.

And he, Evel Knievel, would be her pilot.

"You always sweat it."

"What?" His train of thought broken, Knievel saw the Harley again as just another motorcycle.

"Everything about her, you sweat it all. The spark plugs, the chain, the throttle, the tires. Everything."

"She's all I've got when I get up there," said Knievel. He was hunched over, checking the engine one last time. A drop of sweat fell on his white jump suit—he wiped it away meticulously.

"I think it's time," said Knievel, "to get this show on the road."

"Amen," said Will.

Geoffrey Mandrake back again, ladies and gentlemen, but nothing much has happened since I last spoke to you from the main amphitheater field. There's still no sign of Evel Knievel or his jumping bike. And the crowd is growing very restless here at Wembley Stadium, where we have at least fourteen thousand spectators. It's a hot afternoon, unbearably uncomfortable. As always, the American daredevil on wheels, the man they've called the Cycle Psycho, is attempting to break his previous records. Today the defier of death will take off from a launching platform at approximately eighty-five miles an hour, catapulting his Harley-Davidson machine across thirteen double-decker British buses, lined up in a row, and down again on a landing platform—for a total distance of one hundred and seventy-five feet. And if he can achieve that, ladies and gentlemen, he will break—

Hold it, I can see Knievel now, he's stepping out into the center of the arena. What a resplendent sight. The American is wearing his famous snow-white skintight leathers. There's red striping on each leg of his trousers, and there is an "X" of stars across his chest. White stars representing the United States of America inside a field of navy blue, the blue trimmed in red striping. You can see the lights reflecting off his diamond cufflinks. He's walking with a cane, ladies and gentlemen, I believe it's his famous twenty-two thousand dollar walking stick, the one with the diamonds encrusted in the head. He's walking with a limp—no doubt acquired during one of his earlier jumps—and yet he's walking with swagger, with panache. I must say, it's an impressive, arrogant sight. Just when the crowd thought Evel Knievel would not show up, that he had backed down, he has made a bravura entrance. He's walking to the lectern set up near his launch-

Evel gripped the microphone much the way he gripped the
handlebars of a motorcycle. "Now just what the hell is going
on around here? . . . Just what the hell has been keeping you
folks for so long?"

If there were any cries from hecklers, they were lost,
totally drowned in the roar of acceptance and adulation that
burst from the British spectators.

Any doubts they might have harbored were now gone,
squashed by his vainglory and haughty attitude. But with the
conceit and the vaunting there was a tongue-in-cheek factor
that made Evel Knievel tolerable. Not only tolerable, but
admirable. And not just admired, but loved and respected
for the way he had done the crowd one better.

He was the King of the Jumpers again, and he felt that cer-
tainty flow through his veins as though it were life-giving
blood.

The crowd quieted. "A lot of people ask me . . ."—he spoke
slowly, turning left and then right, then back to center again,
so that they could all get a good look at him and feel as
though he were addressing each of them individually—". . .
they ask me if I have a death wish. Hell no, I don't have a
death wish. Nobody wants to die. We all want to live. But
when you've done what I've done, you've got to have an
extra excitement. And pretty soon jumping across the sky
takes the place of car racing, skiing, even parachute jumping. I live to face that challenge on a daily basis. And I'm
going to face it again today and I'm going to *beat* it again
today."

Knievel dropped the microphone, threw his arms skyward
and stepped off like a bantam rooster, turning to meet Will,
who was wheeling the Harley toward the center of the amphitheater. The crowd was going crazy, loving every moment of
showmanship and spectacle that epitomized Evel Knievel
whenever he lurked on the periphery of a jump.

Knievel stood under the hot afternoon London sun and
took the Harley, winking at Will. "Thanks, old buddy."

"What goes up has got to come down," Will reminded him.
"Just make damn sure you do it on the landing ramp. I don't
want to see you busted up again."

"You and me both."

Knievel gripped the cross-braced handlebars, which he

preferred to call ape-hangers since he had always felt like a gorilla when he gripped them during his descents, knowing full well that if his hands slid . . . no use worrying about that now . . .

Knievel adjusted his leather gloves one final time, strapped on the white crash helmet adorned with stars and threw his right leg across the leather seat. While he could honestly say that most of the features of the three-hundred-and-sixty-pound Harley were factory-produced and not custom-fashioned, it was not true of the seat. It had been designed to absorb extra shock during the hard landings to prevent damage to his buttocks and spine. Too much impact could collapse him like a marionette doll.

Knievel was a solid hundred and eighty pounds, towering to one inch over six feet in height. There was a strong sense of presence, of self-assuredness, that prevented most blowhards from challenging his virility in barrooms across America. There was nothing about him that might have repelled women, however. If anything, he appealed to them with his well-tanned skin (the result of hours of riding in the sun) and his ruggedly handsome features that some had compared to Elvis Presley's. The likable face was topped by wavy blond hair, which in some places was already showing signs of premature gray. It contributed a certain "distinguished" look. His boyish smile was always a surprising contrast to his glib tongue.

But beneath that exterior was no ordinary body. It was a patchwork of mended bones (some of them re-re-mended), a labyrinth of repaired flesh, sewn-together organs and rejuvenated blood.

At one time Evel Knievel had been the closest living thing to the Bionic Man with the working parts to prove it, even if they had not cost six million dollars to install. A giant steel plate had once been screwed into his hip and pelvis and he had been made pliable by screws, bolts, nuts and pins. These surgically implanted steel plates had given him external normalcy, while underneath he had groaned and clanked a metallic cadence with each footfall.

Although the plate and the screws and the bolts and the nuts and the pins had been removed, he still walked with a slight limp. Not every bone and organ in his body had been damaged during his marathon jumps, but the count was enough to stagger any doctor: crushed knee, compounded fracture of the left arm, broken wrist, shattered collarbone, mashed shoulder, splintered ribs, staved lung, brain concussion, compounded fracture of the right leg, chipped and cracked teeth, fractured pelvis, ruptured spleen, pulverized hips, burst lower spine.

The miracle of medical science held his body together, and the magic of his own soulful optimism and philosophical rationalizations held him together spiritually.

That and the Machine.

With his left hand, Knievel squeezed the clutch just before moving the gearshift lever with his foot. He released the clutch and hit the throttle.

He was moving.

He scooted toward the far right end of the stadium, his own personal thoughts accelerated and lost in the explosion of the Harley's forward thrust.

The tail pipes were a glowing red that almost resembled clots of blood shooting out into his wake. He kept building speed, reaching a top of sixty before purposely skidding and sliding the Harley into a hundred-and-eighty-degree turn so he was headed back the way he had just jetted from. It caught the crowd by surprise and they cheered in anticipation of better stunts to come.

He began his standard "warm-up" wheelies—raising up on his front tire so high that everyone swore the Harley was going to overturn and crush him. Three hundred and sixty pounds of bone-grinding weight was enough to make anyone blanch. But as he jerked the wheel, he also hit the throttle, and the Harley shot forward, coming down on the front wheel with such perfection that any noise of contact with the ground was lost in the cacophony of engine sounds that ricocheted off the amphitheater walls.

Performing a "wheelie" was a reflexive, instinctive ritual to Knievel, as common to the warm-up as putting on gloves and leathers, and it hardly occupied his full attention. Which allowed him time to focus on the launching pad and the touch-down ramp.

They were each made of smooth-sanded hardwood, inspected carefully before each jump. The slightest sliver, ridge, bump or depression in the wood could be fatal. The hardwood was supported by steel braces. It was painted a blue that had begun to chip and fade. He made a mental note to have Will repaint them before the next jump. He studied the landing ramp, structured identically to the launch pad except for the fact that instead of being thirty-six feet long, it was extended an extra twenty feet and was marked by long scars burned in by exhaust pipes—remnants of past jumps successfully completed.

Between the ramps were thirteen double-decker buses. He counted them vigilantly, feeling uneasy about the fact there was no Datsun panel truck at the end of the row nearest the touch-down ramp. Having a Datsun in that key position was a prerequisite to his stateside jumps, but would have looked totally out of place among the buses, and he had told Will to forget it.

The Datsun was important because should his engine fail in mid flight, or should he fail to maintain the precarious balance the Harley required once in flight, it was very likely he would land on the last car. And a Datsun had give.

Forget it, he told himself. You aren't going to come down early.

Now, get on with it.

Time to fly.

The audience seemed to sense that he had made up his mind to make the run. The cheering and the applause died away to a whisper and the people who were away from their seats paused, frozen where they were, afraid they would miss the thing they had waited so long to see.

They were all his now. Palm-of-the-hand time. Got you where I want you.

Knievel began his concentration. For an average ten-car jump he would approach the takeoff ramp at fifty miles an hour in second gear, but this was a bigger jump. This would call for eighty-five or ninety miles per hour in third gear. He checked off the key points at the far end of the amphitheater, revving his engine.

Hit the ramp . . . be sure you're standing up . . . lean forward on the pegs . . . the Harley'll have a tendency to buck and want to come over backward on you, so lean forward to hold it down . . . gotta hold that motherbuckin' bronco down . . . go off the ramp right at the top of the power curve . . . travel straight through the air . . . if you're off power, even slightly, the Harley'll drift sideways in the air and get all crossed up.

And you'll get Messed Up.

You got to grab and go you got to gas that cycle that mother that baby that mean machine that lovely flying XR 750 and don't let go hell no man don't let go grip those ape-hangers speed doesn't get you distance. You got to get it right on top of the power curve . . . on top of the power curve don't forget that, you madman genius gladiator daredevil best-there-is-in-the-whole-damn world right at the peak so the rear wheel is driving fast off that chain like a guy crouching and springing up you got to get up on the footpegs on the balls of your feet, hang on and guide this baby through the air if you see you're going to miss, be sure to grit your goddamn teeth you idiot, the people are going to die if you miss that thing what the hell are you saying you're going to die and then the bastards're going to cheer their lungs out shout their uvulas all the way to the Tower of London while you turn into a pile of mush and they scrape you into a gunny sack.

Knievel climbed the ramp at eighty-five miles an hour, leaning into the onrush of air that seemed to enfold and engulf him. Despite the noise of the Harley, he was aware of the hushed, awesome silence that greeted his plunge into mid air.

He floated.

It was a short-lived feeling. For now he was soaring. He felt the thrust of the engine, the surge of the machine.

He was an eagle. Free from the world which had spawned him, from the parents who had procreated him, from the spectators who had made him rich, from the dumb brutish driving fearless force that had made him a defier of everything mortal man feared.

Then came Harmony.

Evel Knievel and the orange machine were as one. Flesh metamorphosed into chrome-plated steel; the throbbing motor pistons transmuted into blood-pumping valves. Man and his mechanical creation were welded, commingled into a single compound that had no divergent purposes.

Each was a part of the other, to be guided and controlled and manipulated for the other's desires. Neither was mightier than the other; yet each was less without the other.

They had ascended together, they had blended their desires and their skills and now each waited for the command of the other.

It was a union born of love and need—man's love for machine, machine's need for man to give it purpose and effect and direction.

It was almost a perfect union.

Almost.

There was disharmony thirty feet above the amphitheater

13

turf. Something incompatible had occurred between man and machine. The coalescing of components was noble, but not Godlike.

There were flaws in each: flaws in the man's manipulation and control of the machine, and in the machine's failure to respond as the man wanted it to respond.

The fusion was broken; the amalgam split asunder into two disparate components, each acting independently, disrespectful of the other.

What had been synthesized harmony was now a mélange of impending disaster.

Knievel felt the rebellion beneath his fingers and in the tendons of his legs—he felt it surge through the seat and vibrate against his buttocks and every other part of his body in contact with the machine.

There was instability and phantasmagoria in all that he felt and saw.

A miscalculation.

An overshoot.

Knievel had the advantage of a singular sensation—of feeling he was suspended in air, not moving forward, not moving backward, but hung in limbo. He knew he really wasn't standing still and yet the paradox of the feeling gave him a moment of crystal clarity, of lucidity he had never felt so vividly before, not even during his worst spills.

It was a realization of what was about to happen.

He saw it clearly now, as though he were a clairvoyant given the power of prescience.

He was going to reach the bottom portion of the landing ramp, but he was going to land off center, at just enough of an angle that a second after impact the front wheel of the Harley would be dropping off the edge of the ramp.

That dip would be enough to throw him out of the saddle headlong into the turf.

Then Knievel was no longer suspended—as though whatever force had held him in place now flung him from its grip and the Harley from the interior of its stomach with an angry regurgitation.

. . . by God, Evel's coming down but he's overshooting the upper portion of the touch-down ramp. He's going to hit hard and he's going . . . he's too far over . . . he's going to hit off center, I can see that from here. He's arcing and dipping . . . the wheel of the Harley has landed with a sharp squeal on the

14

ramp and . . . my God, Evel's motorcycle has plunged off the rampway and he's been thrown from the seat of the bike . . . oh my God, he's being flipped head over heels . . . he's still hurtling through the air. The bike is crashing into the wall. And Evel continues to skid. Like a top he's skidding across the turf. Flung like a rag doll . . . my God, no mortal man could survive such punishment. He's still rolling. Like a kingpin in a bowling alley . . . being tossed and turned and thrown with such incredible velocity. He's finally coming to a stop . . . what an incredible sight, ladies and gentlemen . . . just incredible. The crowd has absolutely gone insane. An ambulance is speeding across the stadium to the aid of the downed daredevil. I can see several figures racing toward Knievel . . . some of them have already reached his body. He isn't moving, I can't tell what's happening from here, but I can only assume he's sustained the worst possible injuries. Perhaps mortal injuries. I just don't know yet and I won't know until we can get a microphone down through the crowd and across the . . . here comes the ambulance, ladies and gentlemen, it's screeching to a halt near Evel's body . . . the motorcycle that crashed against the wall is on fire now, but one of the emergency firemen has raced to the wall and is putting it out with a hand extinguisher. What an event. Listen to that crowd going wild . . . I don't believe it, I just don't believe it. But Evel Knievel is up. Yes, that's right, he's standing up, he's pushing away the nearest ambulance attendant. I can see him shaking his head . . . he is refusing any help. What an incredible sight . . . I can hardly hear myself speak over the roar of the crowd. In all my years of sporting events I've never heard an audience responding like this one. Incredible . . . Evel Knievel is standing fully upright . . . I just don't believe it, not after seeing that tremendous fall he took moving at eighty miles an hour or more. What a gesture of unforgettable gallantry, ladies and gentlemen, as Evel Knievel pushes aside the ambulance attendants and doctors and stands alone. He's all by himself now, standing there, barely able to move, reeling, weaving from side to side . . . one of the doctors moved toward Knievel just now but he's waved him away. And now he's turning to face the spectators. He's raising his hands to tell the audience that he's all right. Listen to that crowd. It's gone absolutely insane. If they came here today to see him bleed, they're seeing it, but they're also seeing him standing there, still taking it, still fighting back the

15

pain. An incredible display of bravery and adversity in the face of death. Absolutely incredible . . .

He felt nothing. Only the heat of the sun.

If there were pain, it was drowned in the accolades resounding throughout the amphitheater. If there was suffering, it was lost in the exaltation he felt surge through him, knowing he had satisfied the fans in more ways they could ever have hoped for.

They had wanted his blood.

He had given them his blood.

It was there for all to see, scattered in tiny pools . . . scattered erratically from the point of bodily impact to where he now stood.

And that was one thing they hadn't counted on: that he would still be standing.

He was aware of perspiration all over his body and he could feel a coolness where his leathers had split at the seams. He lost more damn leathers this way.

He'd said it before. He'd say it again. "I'm incomparable. I'm the greatest."

And the crowd kept on cheering.

2

Interview

WHAT *other famous daredevils would you compare yourself to, Mr. Knievel?*

Evel, call me Evel, ole buddy. There's nothing in the world formal enough you should have to call me "Mister." A lot of journal jocks have asked me that question. I always tell 'em the same thing. I don't like to compare myself to other men. I'm unique among men. There hasn't been anyone like me before, there won't be anyone like me after. Some good fellas have tried, and they're either pushing daisies in serene locations or they're doing wheelies in wheelchairs in the old folks' home, waiting for their bones to knit so they can take up an easy line of work—like selling sewing machines or manufacturing Frisbees or looking for four-leaf clovers on a Sunday afternoon picnic.

How exactly are you feeling today?

I'm feeling great because I am great. Any day I get out of a hospital is a great day, ole buddy. In my line of work, you can't lay around in these places too long. Got to heal and knit so I can get back out there on the field and make another jump. Keep those fans happy and yellin' for more of the same.

They tell me you watched a lot of television during your convalescence. How does British television compare to the programs in America?

You've got better heroes in this country.

Better heroes?

Dr. Who, he's my favorite.

Why Dr. Who? Surely you have your own superheroes in America.

Ah, nuts to the Bionic Woman and all those other creeps. They're just like me, trapped in the twentieth century. No way to go forward or back. But Dr. Who's the greatest of

17

them all, inventing new contraptions. He's also the greatest explorer of them all. He's able to return to the past in his time machine. Or he can zoom into the future.

Why do you find that so appealing?

Whether it's in the past or the present, there're new frontiers to conquer. Today we live in an age when there aren't any frontiers, when the explorers have had to come to a standstill. See, we've conquered our planet, ole buddy, and here we are, waitin' for the chance to get out there in space and conquer all those other solar systems and star systems. A million different places out there, but here we are, stuck in neutral, jacked up on blocks with our wheels spinning to nowhere, waiting for the NASA boys to get things moving again. So that's why I admire Dr. Who—he can travel to all those planets and solar systems and galaxies and milky ways and win them over. Me, I'm stuck here on the planet earth. So that's why I have to jump, ole buddy. It'd be a bore if I didn't jump.

Soothsayers in the sporting world are predicting you might try Indianapolis.

Bad scan, Englishman. Indianapolis is a great place, don't get me wrong. It's wonderful. But I don't want to join the numbers, the ranks, and fall in line with a mess of other guys all doing the same trip. Pulling the same number. I want to do something that's never been done before. Auto racers, they defy death. Me, I stare it in the face—sometimes I spit right in its eye. Ole buddy, I believe we were all born dead. I didn't ask to be put here on earth. I've accepted the fact that dying is a part of living. I don't know if what I'm doing is going to make a worthwhile contribution to society or transportation, but I'm going to do it. I'm going to keep on jumping.

What about your body? Can it continue to take the kind of abuse it withstood at Wembley last month?

The body is no different from a precision-made machine. As long as you keep oiling the parts, replacing the broken and mended and cracked, it'll hold together. A little Elmer's Glue never hurts, either. Maybe it won't hold forever, but at least for the lifetime of the guarantee.

And your guarantee?

A hundred years or fifty thousand jumps. Whichever comes first.

What are your plans now, Evel?

I'm headed back for the most beautiful country in the

world. The United States of America. I've got a jump to perform for the Long Beach crowd. They love my kind of act in California.

One last question, Evel. I know you're anxious to get to the airport . . . but how did it feel as you were headed down the take-off ramp at Wembley?

The hardest problem is making sure you don't lose your nerve just before you jump. Hell, I didn't have a problem at Wembley. I had a situation. I'm always positive I can jump because if a man honestly conceives an idea and honestly believes it, and he wants to do the thing badly enough, he'll do it. Nothing in the world can stop him.

Just why do you do it, Evel? Why do you go racing down that launching platform?

Simple, ole buddy. To get to the other side.

3

Sentimental Slob

I T was not the night before Christmas. But something was stirring in the Charity Hills Orphanage.

On the third floor, moving as silently as a burglar, limping under the weight of the huge red sack heaved over his shoulder, Evel Knievel cursed under his breath for forgetting to bring a flashlight. He cursed above his breath when his instincts failed him and he banged gracelessly against a wall at a turn in the corridor.

The pain in his hip and left leg were intensified by the unexpected encounter, and the bag over his shoulder wasn't helping. He placed the sack on the floor with a light thud, wiped the sweat from his forehead and chin, and continued to maneuver through the darkness, but with greater care. He was wearing a checked tan jacket, maroon shirt and pants and tan leather boots.

If the cynics of the world could have seen Knievel at that moment, they would have called him a sentimental slob. A soft touch, a chump, a jerk with a heart of gold.

If Knievel could have heard the cynics of the world, he would have told them all to go to hell.

He reached the double swinging doors and, without pausing, barged his way through, relieved to have reached his destination and no longer concerned with silence or secrecy.

He found the dormitory in almost complete darkness. Two rows of beds faced each other in stark, geometric, institutional harshness.

Danny slept the sleep of a ten-year-old, his tousled hair and contented face saintly in its slumbering innocence.

Knievel placed the red bag on the floor, its weight creating another light thud.

The youth stirred, his head burrowing into the pillow. Slowly his eyes opened. Slowly his eyes closed.

And blinked open again.

It was gaping, youthful wonderment that greeted Knievel. The pain in his leg and hip, and the discomfort to his shoulder caused by the sack, were forgotten as Danny came completely awake. To Knievel, the boy was the most beautiful creature on God's earth, and he defied anyone to tell him otherwise.

"Evel!"

"Hiya Danny."

The figure that Danny saw was not a swaggering, brash man, not a flippant, hard-drinking daredevil who flew as high on bull as he did on a Harley-Davidson.

The figure that Danny saw was, instead, a kind, generous, sensitive man, whose kindness knew no bounds, whose generosity was sincere.

To Danny, Knievel was the ultimate hero, the final towering image of manhood, commanding the utmost respect and adulation.

Knievel looked into Danny's face and saw the recognition of his largess, and he silently cursed the need for orphanage homes.

The youth in the next bed stirred. "Is that really you, Mr. Knievel?"

"Evel, son, all my friends call me Evel."

"I can't believe it," cried Danny. "You're really here."

"Said I'd be, didn't I?"

Young eyes widened, almost bulged, as Knievel untied the red bag and reached inside. What he brought out were the riches of the young: skateboards, Planet of the Apes gameboards, pencil puzzle books, boxes containing the Evel Knievel Trail Bike, the Evel Knievel Stunt World Set, the Evel Knievel Funny Car, the Evel Knievel Super Cycle, Tonka trucks, Earthmovers, fire engines, ambulances, dump trucks, Vertibird Paramedic Rescue Sets, the Hot Wheels Double-Dual Speedway, slot car sets, Hang Man, the Bermuda Triangle Game, Jaws, Air Trix, Worm Wrestle, Twister, Body Language, Numbers Up and Perfection.

Knievel began passing them out, and soon the entire ward was roused and alive and bug-eyed as the gifts circulated from bed to bed; as young homeless boys came to experience a new sensation.

"I told the guys you wouldn't forget," said Danny.

"I got held up for a little while, Danny. Took a little spill on the bike. You know how slow those damn doctors are."

"Yeah, I know."

An eleven-year-old boy named Pete lunged forward to throw his arms around Knievel.

"Hey, go easy on me, tiger. Ease off, big fella."

They were rushing to surround Knievel now, feeling out to make certain he was real and not another of their unfulfilled dreams.

What their fingertips felt was sugar and spice.

"Hey," whispered a boy named Scott, who was opening a Scrabble game box, "keep the noise down. Let's not spoil the fun."

The excited voices dropped to excited murmurs.

"I forgot about your accident," remarked Pete. "How're you feeling?"

"How do I look?" asked Knievel, flexing his muscles and smiling.

"Super." Pete grinned as wide a grin as Evel had ever seen in a boy so young.

"That's me. Super Knievel."

"Where you comin' from, Evel?"

"I saw you on TV. Man, were you neat."

"Don't make noise, guys."

"Keep it down. If Mother Superior hears us . . ."

"Thanks for the game, Evel. It's swell."

"Hey, Evel, look at this."

Knievel turned to see a boy of twelve with a cast on his left leg, hobbling from the far end of the dormitory on crutches. He was slow, he moved with trepidation and hesitancy, but he was moving. The boy's pride was apparent in his glowing eyes and face.

"That's Wally," said Danny, "he's been that way for a long time."

Wally threw away one of his crutches with an air of disdain, but he maintained his balance. He took a step forward. He teetered, but he didn't fall. "When I saw you walk away from that crash in England," said Wally, "I figured I could walk too."

Knievel moved off Danny's bed to place his hands on Wally's shoulders and look the boy fully in the face.

"You're the reason I'm walking, Evel."

"That's great," said Knievel. "I knew you could do it." He slapped his knee in jubilation. "I'm so proud of you. So proud."

23

"Where's your next jump going to be. Evel?" That was a boy named Russ.

"Long Beach."

"Is it gonna be televised?"

"Maybe."

"How about putting on another show for us?" That was a boy named Billy.

"Gonna have breakfast with us like last time?" Howie.

"You can umpire our baseball game on Saturday." Jerry.

"We want you to stay for a long time." Andy.

"Please say you'll stay, Evel." Larry.

By now the youthful voices had returned to their full volume; caution was forgotten in the excitement of the moment. So Knievel wasn't at all surprised when the lights in the dormitory came on in a sudden burst of brilliance. To the boys, it had the sting of an ice cold shower.

Nor was Knievel surprised at the sight of Sister Charity standing just inside the double doors, her hands planted firmly against her sides in a holier-than-thou attitude. That holiness was lost when her mouth fell open. "What the devil . . ." Her voice was the essence of outrage, but controlled outrage.

"Not the devil, Sister."

"Knievel!" There was still a note of outrage, but he detected that it was feigned. Or was it?

"Haven't changed a bit, Sister Charity," he said grinning, jumping off Danny's bed. "You're still the prettiest thing that ever joined the Church."

She tried to ignore that, but he suspected that her toes, if he could have seen them, were turning a scarlet red. "None of your blarney, Evel Knievel. What are you doing here in the middle of the night? Waking the boys out of a sound sleep . . . arriving uninvited."

"And unannounced," added Knievel. They had been through this routine before. He never tired of it. He suspected Sister Charity felt the same way about it.

Under other circumstances, in another place, Knievel might have fallen for Sister Charity. She was young, not more than thirty-five, and she had a lovely, almost angelic, face. He was uncertain about the rest of her, but he suspected that hidden beneath that habit was a figure just as gorgeous. That was something, he decided, that he would never know for sure.

"Well, I made a little promise to the boys, Sister. Promised

24

I'd come see them first thing after getting back from Britain."

"That's no excuse for the misconduct of these children." She turned sternly to the boys, spoke sharply, uncompromisingly. "I want you all in bed immediately. Now. Fast."

They scrambled to obey. They clutched their gifts to their bodies and dived for their beds. Wally limped his way back on his crutches, swinging more freely now, as one inspired.

"And you, Mr. Knievel," scolded Sister Charity, "I'd like to have a talk with you."

Evel leaned down and scooped up the red sack, which was conspicuously close to empty. He winked one final time at Danny, who winked back, and then followed Sister Charity out into the corridor.

She glared at him. He ran his eyes down the habit, hoping for some glimpse of what was beneath. He could see nothing except what he was supposed to see.

"Darn you, Evel, you could have waited until morning."

"Wouldn't have been as exciting," he said teasingly. "Besides, things look different in daylight."

"Still playing Santa Claus?"

"Tomorrow I have to be in Long Beach."

"Why didn't you say so?"

"You forgot to ask . . . say, I picked up something . . ." Knievel reached down into the red sack and brought up a gaily wrapped, narrow box of candy. He extended it to Sister Charity. "Picked up your favorite fudge when I was in New York. Here, take it, enjoy."

She looked at the gift not unlike the way Danny had looked at the red sack. Finally she accepted it, her expression changing to one of guilt. "I'll get fat."

"Eat hearty, Sister. It'll never show."

The serenity was gone from her manner and the glare was gone from her face when she said, "Thank you, Brother Knievel."

"Thank *you*, Sister Charity."

"And God bless you," she added.

Knievel took her arm and led her along the corridor. He had purposely left the red sack outside the double doors of the dormitory.

It would be something extra for the boys to remember in the morning.

4

The Champ Returns

E VEL Knievel had come to feel an affinity for the people of Long Beach during earlier jumps, and it was no coincidence that he chose that California city for his triumphant return to the United States following his spectacular, if injurious, jump at Wembley Stadium.

A huge white banner was stretched across the main entrance to the vast Long Beach Veterans Stadium, its red lettering proclaiming: WELCOME EVEL KNIEVEL—WORLD RECORD JUMP JULY 23.

If the sign provided some hint of Knievel's popularity, the crowd that had gathered verified it. It consisted of several fans of all ages; of photographers, news cameramen, reporters and television crews. The playing field was studded with multicolored balloons; red, white and blue bunting on the face of the bleachers; and streamers which heralded earlier jumps made by Knievel. Sexy pom-pom girls danced wildly and cheered to the inspiring music of a high-school band decked out in full regalia.

It was an unusual afternoon for July: balmy and cool, smogless, with a nice sea breeze.

Three Long Beach Police Department black-and-whites were parked nearby, but the patrolmen were relaxed, for it was not an unruly crowd. On the contrary, it was respectfully patient, knowing that it had only a few more minutes of forbearance before the Grand Arrival.

The city of Long Beach had been given a hero, and fittingly it had turned out to greet him.

A white Cadillac pick-up, with two Harley-Davidsons loaded in the bed, drove onto the playing field, its engine revving, and the crowd started to applaud. The band began a new song, the girls danced with renewed excitement, and

27

cameras were aimed. The crowd surged toward the Cadillac.

"Knievel!"

"Is that him? He doesn't look like no jumper to me."

"There he is. Hey, Evel."

"That isn't Knievel, you idiot. Just some schnook."

"I bet he's part of Evel's entourage."

"I never saw him before. He must be nobody."

The applause and the dancing and the music and the cries of worship died away and the crowd, disappointed, returned to its tolerant vigil.

The pick-up jerked to a stop and Will Atkins, wearing mechanic's coveralls and a cap pulled tightly down over his eyes, climbed out, squinting across the playing field at a man who stood at the far end of the stadium, near a stack of folding chairs, talking to a workman.

Will scowled, slammed the door of the Cadillac and stepped off angrily. "Ben Andrews!" he screamed.

Andrews turned. He was a few years younger than Will, about five foot seven, one hundred and fifty pounds. There was a certain dapper quality about him, a twinkle in his eye. He wore flashy clothing: checkered coat, striped pants, a colorful handkerchief carefully knotted at the throat, and a straw hat. He might have passed for a carnival barker.

Ben Andrews acknowledged Will with a barely audible grunt and continued to listen to the construction worker. "But Mr. Andrews, we can't put up seats on the infield. We'd be blocking the north exit."

Ben Andrews struck his own forehead with the palm of his hand. "Are you blind? We've got an exit. The main one."

The workman shook his head disapprovingly. "But if there's an emergency, you're going to need more than one way for everyone to clear out."

'Listen, you punk, don't talk back to me. You were hired to put up those seats. Do it or I'll get someone else who will without any questions asked." By now Andrews was punching a finger against the chest of the workman and looking at him as though he were dirt.

"Ben Andrews!"

Will continued his rapid approach. His walk had the foreboding of a storm. But Andrews didn't seem to notice—or pretended not to notice.

"Now get to work, punk," said Andrews scornfully to the workman. "Get lost and don't let me see you again until those chairs are in position." The workman slinked away.

28

Ben Andrews gave Will his full attention now, turning to proffer his hand. Will brushed it aside and grabbed Ben by the shoulders and slammed him violently against the wall of the grandstand. There was a slur in Will's voice and a flush to his face that told Andrews the mechanic had been drinking heavily.

"Hiya pal," said Andrews.

"Hiya pal," mimicked Will sarcastically. "You're all through trying to get Evel knocked off," he raged.

Andrews' startled surprise turned to confoundedness. "Killed? What the hell're you talking about? Have you gone whacky again?"

Andrews tried to pull himself free, but Will's grip was unbreakable. Andrews saw over Will's shoulder that Knievel's Stutz was swinging onto the playing field, stopping next to the Cadillac, and the crowd was surrounding the daredevil

"Listen to me," growled Will. "Evel needs more room."

"I'm giving him room."

"Mud in the sink is what you've been giving him. At the last jump there were bleacher seats right on the field."

"Ease off, you crazy gorilla. Evel's my bread and butter too."

"He's more than bread and butter to me. All you care about is filling your own pockets with blood money. I'll give odds you're gonna put seats on this infield. Well, if I see any bleachers there, I'll make kindling out of them. And set fire to your ass along with them."

"Get your gorilla fingers off me, Will. The stadium owner sold those seats."

"He what?"

"I didn't sell them."

"You're a goddamn liar."

"It's the truth."

"It's crap."

"Give me a break."

"I'll break your neck. I know you're lying, Ben, because I've already checked it out."

Grasping Andrews with his left hand, Will pulled back his right arm to deliver a punch to the promoter. It was at that moment that Knievel reached the two men, coming between them, his powerful arms separating the two. The crowd cheered. As usual, Knievel was giving them more than they had bargained for.

"Sorry about this, Ben," said Knievel soothingly.

"Keep this gorilla of yours off me, Evel. If you can't keep him in his cage, I'll find someone who will." Ben Andrews sucked in his stomach indignantly and stormed away toward one of the exits. Only after the promoter was out of sight did Knievel lessen his grip on Will.

"Now you're picking fights," Knievel said accusingly.

"You don't even know what happened."

"It doesn't make any difference what happened. You can't straighten it out here. I know one thing, you're putting on a bad show for the public."

"As long as you're involved, Evel, there isn't anything they don't applaud. Far as they're concerned, this is part of the show."

"Whatever's eating you, Will, get hold on yourself. This is no place to settle your differences with Ben."

A roaring filled their ears and they turned. Onto the field behind Knievel and Will came two tractor-trailer rigs—the final arriving vehicles in what was known as "The S.S. Knievel." One was the equipment truck, which housed all the jump bikes, Will's tools and spare parts, one white golf cart and bag, several tons of steel ramps and other paraphernalia needed for the death-defying leaps. The forward cab-over diesel had a fourteen-speed Allison automatic transmission.

The second rig was in keeping with the design of a recreational vehicle—but it was uniquely Knievel, having been custom-designed for his living and office quarters by Kenworth of Kansas City at a cost of $140,000.

The crowd came forward now, swarming around Knievel. The photographers looked like determined soldiers armed with weapons as they leveled their cameras and began shooting more pictures.

"I'll see what we've got in the treasure chest for the kids," remarked Will, moving toward the equipment rig.

Police officers moved in to make sure the fans weren't pressing too hard. Knievel grinned at them and the cops got the message, stepping back. He'd call them if things got out of hand.

Programs were thrust at Knievel and he signed as many as he could. Photographers shouted for him to look their way. He obliged as best he could, patting some of the children on the head, shaking an occasional adult hand, returning comment for comment. There was no mistaking his acceptance of their hero worship. He was eating it up and he wasn't hiding the good taste it left in his mouth.

Knievel made a point of asking for names, so that his autographs would be personalized. A reporter made his way to Knievel, notebook and ballpoint pen in hand. Even before he spoke, Knievel asked, "What journal you jocking for?"

"*Long Beach Press-Telegram*. Name's Heath. Evel, what's your comment on the big jump Jessie Hammond made in Tampa?"

"Jessie who?" He was clowning and the crowd knew it and it broke everyone up.

Heath was a man of persistence. "A lot of people think that Jessie is pushing you hard for the number one spot."

"Well," said Knievel graciously, still signing autographs, "Jessie's a good kid and a fine jumper. But he's no Knievel."

The crowd applauded. Right on, right on.

Knievel just kept on signing. "And when you're not Knievel, you're not number one." He turned to face the crowd. "Isn't that right?"

The crowd's response was predictable. It agreed.

"Is it true you and Jessie had a falling out once—back when he was working for you?" Heath started scribbling notes even before Knievel replied.

"Jessie was always falling out—of the saddle of his Honda."

More raucous laughter, a smattering of applause.

A gorgeous brunette, wearing a halter top that was pointedly revealing and a pair of flaming red hotpants, worked her way to the front of the crowd. It was pretty obvious, judging by the smile on her face, what she had in mind.

The brunette brushed some of the hair out of her blinking baby-blue eyes and asked, "Can I tell you what to write on the photo?"

"Honey," purred Knievel, "I've known what to say ever since kindergarten."

As soon as the laughter had died away, the brunette pointed to the large diamond ring he wore. "That's some ring, Evel," she said, awed.

"That's no ring, sweetheart. That's a portable TV."

Knievel raised his hand until the ring was directly in front of her lovely face. "Tune in your favorite channel, honey."

"Go ahead," shouted a photographer, "pretend it's a TV."

"Tune in 'Let's Make a Deal,'" shouted one of the children.

The brunette reached up and pretended to twist the diamond. "I don't see any picture," she said saucily.

"Gee," said Knievel, "I must not be receiving today."

In the rear of the equipment van, Will took a quart of Bourbon De Luxe from the wooden chest and downed a hearty mouthful of Kentucky straight bourbon whiskey, eighty proof. He returned the half-empty bottle to the chest, wedging it down among the stacks of Evel Knievel T-shirts and jump posters. It was the one place Knievel would never think of looking. He picked up a handful of merchandise from the "treasure chest" but paused before moving toward the open doors.

He sighed and felt a warmth from the bourbon, and a calmness came over him—a rare feeling these days for Will Atkins. His argument with Ben Andrews was almost forgotten now. Maybe he had made a fool of himself, but sometimes that's what it took to keep Evel from getting killed because some rip-off promoter only cared about the number of seats he sold, not about the safety of the jumper.

It was dumb because if the jumper were maimed or killed he would never jump again and there would be no more seats to sell. But try to explain the logic of that to a promoter—he never saw beyond tomorrow's deal. Ben Andrews had to be the most short-sighted individual who ever existed.

Maybe he and Knievel were the short-sighted ones. Busting their asses all the time to give the people a thrill. Knievel had often questioned if any of this had any lasting value—and Will had often questioned it too. Every day of his life. Only now he didn't want to question it any more. He wanted to forget it.

Forgetting was Will's way of making it through the day. Forget the problems of the morning and he could make it through the afternoon. Forget the problems of the afternoon and he could have a bearable night—if the bottle of bourbon wasn't too far away.

So it went for Will Atkins, every day, so that the years dragged by, each indistinguishable from the others.

Never forgive . . . just forget. He glanced down into the "treasure chest" at the bottle of Bourbon De Luxe. There was the helper.

Norman Clark, a sandy-haired, blue-eyed, slightly built man of thirty in a wrinkled gabardine suit, was one of the photographers surrounding Knievel, but anyone watching him closely would have noticed that his interest was not so much in Knievel as in the equipment rig.

While everyone's attention was focused on Knievel, he snapped the rig from every conceivable angle. He was standing near the open doors of the van when Will Atkins emerged carrying T-shirts and jump posters. Clark was crossing the field to return to his car when a helicopter swooped low over the empty stadium and set down dead center on the playing field. He slung his camera over his shoulder, whistling in the mood of a man who had just finished a job to his thorough satisfaction.

5

Grand Entrance

KATE Morgan was a knockout. She was chic and elegant, poised and confident—a regal creature with a regal body, a regal bearing and a regal ability to tell men where to get off. If anything, they loved her more for it. It was evident, just from the way she moved, that Kate was a girl who knew where she had been, where she was going, and how she was going to get there.

She wasn't thirty yet, but she had already accomplished more than some men accomplish in a lifetime.

If anyone would have told her that, she would have told them to get lost. Politely, of course. Politeness was always her way with people who bored her.

Boredom is what had given her two professions. She had begun her career at seventeen as a fashion model, working for the House of Dior for fifty dollars a week. By nineteen she was the acknowledged leader in her field, described as "the greatest mannequin in history." Her face adorned the covers of *Vogue, Glamour, Ladies Home Journal*. She sold some of TV's most elegant perfumes and deodorants. Within those two years she had become the darling of the jet set, the paparazzi's delight.

The paparazzi didn't care when Kate told them to push off. She would still pose for their cameras. That was the thing about Kate. She had ideals and standards, yet she didn't allow them to get in her way on a day-to-day basis.

If a paparazzi asked her to hike her skirt a little higher to show off more of her beautiful legs, she just might do it. To shake up the fellas back home, if for no other reason.

Then came the boredom. The indifference to jet-setting, to villas on the Riviera where even the loose patterns of love-making and orgiastic combinations weren't enough to hold her interest beyond six months. By the time she was twenty-five she was bored stiff. Kate did not like to be predictable, she had too much ambition in her for the humdrum.

So, not unlike Evel Knievel, she had sought the adventurous, the dangerous, the compelling. She found them by switching to the other side of the camera.

By accepting the most perilous, she received assignments from national and foreign magazines, and swiftly gained a brilliant reputation.

She had climbed Everest with a French expedition; she had learned downhill skiing so she could mount a camera atop her headgear and film some spectacular footage; she had photographed the great white shark with Peter Benchley off the shores of the Great Barrier Reef of Australia.

Kate proved that she had courage as well as talent, and the numbers of people she had to tell to screw themselves diminished. It didn't matter to her any longer what people said. Most people were inane and fatuous to begin with; it wasn't worth the waste of her breath any longer.

She was the superior of most men, and refused to consider even the remotest possibility of marriage.

But Kate had lost none of her glamour, none of her sophistication, none of her poise, none of the sexiness and earthiness that broadcast itself whenever she made the slightest move.

Evel Knievel was aware that he was watching an unusual woman as Kate stepped off the helicopter. Suddenly he was no longer thinking only of the crowd. All he could think about, and see, was Kate as she moved toward him.

She was a lioness on tawny legs, stalking the veldt for her latest kill. Her camera case was slung over one shoulder, yet it did not spoil the glamorous effect her clothing and complexion radiated.

Kate, in keeping with all she had learned as one of the nation's leading fashion models, had been poured into a custom-made tunic with matching pants of double-knit polyester. It was Sherwood green, and it reminded Knievel of fresh fields of unmown grass, of leaves touched slightly by the wind. The tunic was pullover-style with open-front placket and a stand-up collar and button-cuffed long sleeves. The tie-belt was a sash of matching material, and even the way she had tied it was sexy, with the loose ends hanging down over her thighs and brushing against them as she walked. The pants had slightly flared legs. Her white open-toed shoes had just enough heel to give her the sexy elevation Knievel preferred.

As Kate moved toward him, registering no reaction to his presence, Knievel realized he was hypnotically zeroed in on her tawny face. The cheeks were flushed a sexy red, the mouth was painted a tantalizing ruby red, and her nose was finely chiseled into streamlined nuances.

Petite silver jewelry adorned her ears. Her hair was free-flowing and natural, cascading around her shoulders.

It was her eyes that kept Knievel entranced: heavily surrounded by eyeshadows so that the whites stood out vividly. Within those fields of white floated two baby-blue irises that could only be described as gorgeous.

Knievel felt a little weak-kneed, and just a little foolish, when Kate walked right past him without any acknowledgment, leaped onto the hood of the Cadillac pick-up, and began snapping pictures of him with her Nikon.

She continued to give him the cold shoulder as Knievel excused himself from the crowd and leaned against the Cadillac, unconcerned that the dust might spoil his leathers. He spoke as flatly as he could. "Thanks for stepping on my entrance. You really know how to take the play away."

"Oh, don't mention it, it comes naturally," said Kate, still refusing to look at Knievel, even if she had acknowledged his voice. "With some of the cheaper acts, it isn't hard at all."

The offensive remark only piqued his interest. He couldn't shake the thought that there was something super-special about this woman. "You must like making enemies, miss."

"*Ms* to you."

"Miss?"

"It's *Ms.* Capital *M*, small *s* . . . hope that isn't too much for you to absorb in one afternoon. Hate to see you blow all your brainpower."

"All stuntmen must be stupid . . . that the way you figure it?"

"Not all. I'm sure if I hang around here long enough I'll meet an intelligent stuntman."

"So," said Knievel, frowning, "you're one of those."

"And that makes you one of *those*." Kate ripped out the exposed rool of film and inserted a fresh one, snapping the camera closed with a certain insolence.

"I'm just a man doing my own thing. Are you a woman or a mmmsssss?"

For the first time Kate looked at Knievel. Goddamn, he thought, I finally cut some ice with her.

"*Mr.* Knievel, chances are you'll never know."

If Knievel was stung, he tried not to let it show. "What makes you think I'd want to find out? You'll do anything to give yourself the edge."

Kate swung her camera on Knievel, snapping a quick series of pictures. "Don't move," she ordered. She jumped down from the Cadillac, moved to his right side, snapped another series. Then to his left. Snap, snap, snap, snap. "From what I've seen of the local competition," she said, "I think I started here with an edge. As a matter of fact, you might even say it's a downright unfair advantage."

"You know," said Knievel, "you're about the biggest blowhard I've ever come across.'

"Takes one to know one, *Mr.* Knievel." She ordered him not to move before he had time to respond. She ducked down in front of him and snapped a series of low angle shots. As she stood upright, he snapped his fingers and smiled at her in sudden recognition.

"The face was familiar all the time, it just took me a while to put it all together." He tapped his forehead self-mockingly. "I must have had a rough night. Sure, you're Kate Morgan. The beautiful Kate Morgan. The fearless photographer who'll go anywhere, do anything."

"Not quite anything, *honey*."

"So the big magazines have sent a chump to shoot a champ."

"With a .375 Magnum Nikon."

Knievel chose to ignore that comment. "You're going to get some great shots of me jumping, *honey*. Miss . . . or should I say *Ms*?" He pronounced the word distinctly and grinned boyishly as he said it.

Kate remained unruffled. She also remained unimpressed.

"Well, you know what? You're still wrong. There're a million shots of you jumping. I'm not here to shoot that. My editors wouldn't let me waste the film. My assignment, in case you're still curious, *Mr.* Knievel, is to photograph you—"

"Well now," said Knievel, easing his stance, "things are looking up."

"—to photograph you just in case this is your last jump."

Knievel frowned. "Who told you I was quitting?"

"That's not what I meant." Kate snapped one last picture, camera atilt, artsy-craftsy style, then swirled and made her way through the crowd toward one of the stadium exits.

"Boy, you're real cute, aren't you," he mumbled. He still had to admire her cool. "What a woman."

Knievel turned back to face the expectant crowd which once again swarmed around him. "Okay, kids, let's get back to what we were doing."

"Will you sign my autograph book, Evel?"

"Sure son."

Now the newspaper reporters homed in on their target.

"Is that the same bike you're using in the big jump?"

"Same one."

"Where's your home town?"

"Montana."

"When're you going to fly over the Canyon again?"

"I never lost anything in the bottom of the Canyon and I'm not going back there."

"What's your physical condition?"

"Super."

"When did they first start calling you Evel?"

"Honey, I was such a good little boy they nicknamed me Evel."

Ben Andrews appeared at the rear of the crowd carrying a golf bag with the initials E.K. engraved in the white leather.

"Excuse me just a minute, folks, here comes my caddy. We have some business to take care of; we'll be right back." He worked his way through the crowd toward Ben, sensing the disappointment. "Excuse us for just a second."

"Are you gonna give us another statement, Evel?"

"I will when I come out. Just keep gripping your papers."

Ben Andrews was starting up the steps of the recreational van when Knievel caught up with him. He helped Ben with the golf bag, patting him gently on the back, hoping he hadn't taken Will's attack too personally.

For a moment, Ben Andrews felt at ease—Knievel's living quarters tended to do that to visitors. It was a resplendent setting, symbolic of his material success. More than one guest had dubbed it a Playboy Club on wheels.

Certainly the combination living quarters–office had all the comforts. It was tastefully decorated in Las Vegas executive: black leather chairs, wall-to-wall carpeting of thick-pile zebra-striped wool, and dark wood paneling that matched a paneled bar well-stocked with the most expensive alcohol, the most exotic mixes and beer on draught.

Since Knievel traveled at least forty thousand miles across country every year, the van was adaptable to the weather: For the hot states an air-conditioning system, for the cold states a thermostatically controlled heating system.

There was a stereo system, color television set, oak desks where Knievel conducted his business. The closets were stuffed with jumping leathers, coveralls and at least a hundred expensive, eye-popping shirts—dress and sport.

Knievel was in the process of propping the golf bag against the massive king-sized bed when Andrews said, "I think your pal Will's reached the end of the road."

Knievel shook his head, sliding an eight iron out of the bag. "Will and me . . . we travel together and we still got a long way to go."

Ben had spoken viciously; Knievel's immediate reaction was to swing the eight iron at an imaginary golf ball.

"You're making a mistake, Evel. Will's a lush, a goddamn drunk. Get rid of him before he gets you killed."

As in all matters regarding Will Atkins, Knievel exhibited nothing but patience—and a concern for his golf stroke.

"You're all worked up, Ben. Relax. No harm'll ever come to me because of Will Atkins."

Andrews was adamant. "He's gonna finish you off some day, Evel, without half trying. Him and his damn bottle." There was malevolence in Andrews' voice, but Knievel's reply was gentle and tempered: "Ben, the clock stopped for Will."

"Ten years ago. You think I've forgotten?"

"Will was the greatest jumper in the world."

"Was. Now he's the greatest boozer."

"He's got his reasons for drinking."

"The dumbest reasons I've ever heard. And believe me, some of the best drunks in the country have told me why they drink."

"Someone's wife dying isn't what I'd call dumb."

"I was talking about his attitude toward his son."

"Tommy?"

"He's got no reason to hate that boy. No business to hold that boy responsible for his wife dying in childbirth."

Knievel slid the eight iron back into the bag. "I don't think Will holds the boy responsible. Not really. He holds himself responsible. For being a thousand miles away the day Tommy was born, jumping and crashing. All in one chuck he became a widower and an ex-champ."

40

"He couldn't take it out on himself enough," said Ben, "so he took it out on the boy. But what the hell're we talking about? None of this is reason for him to stomp on me today. Am I right or am I right?"

"Try to understand, Ben. Everything I've got is because of Will Atkins. He taught it all to me. Every time I ride, the crowd should be cheering him as well as me. So don't let it bug you, Ben. Now, let's get down to business here. What's in the bag?"

Andrews turned the golf bag upside down. Huge stacks of money, bundled together by rubber bands, fell onto the floor. Knievel whistled—he never seemed to get over the excitement of seeing so much money come out of such a small bag. "What's the total?"

Ben scratched his nose, equally pleased at the sight of so much cash. "Forty-two thousand five hundred . . . half your advance. Same guarantee you asked for. You got it."

"You're a little short, aren't you, Ben?" asked Knievel, almost casually, certainly not accusingly.

Ben's jaw drooped—was he startled or indignant? "It's all there, Evel. Count it. I counted it twice. It's all there, I tell you."

"Sure," said Knievel casually, sprawling across the bed and propping his head up with his hands. "It's all there. Except for my share of those bleacher seats you personally sold at the last jump."

Andrews exploded. For a moment, Knievel thought he was going to swing a punch. But Andrews knew better. All right to mouth off all he wanted, but physical force? . . . well, he knew better when Knievel was around.

"What is this, Evel? Judgment Day?"

"You're the one making judgments, Ben."

"I'm good and sick and tired of having rocks thrown at me. I've taken all I'm going to take from this outfit."

"That's right, Ben, stand on your own two feet."

"First that falling-down boozehound buddy of yours braces me. And now you. Well, back off, mister."

"I'm back, Ben," said Knievel, holding his arms into the air. "I'm not crowding you."

"You're not my judge and jury. I didn't kill anyone."

Knievel was the coolest cat in the world, when any other man would have been outraged. "That's right, you didn't kill anyone. *Yet.* Just keep selling seats where I need landing room and let's see what happens. Yeah, Ben, you didn't kill anyone. But you did *steal from me*." A certain iciness had pervaded his voice. He got icier: "But if you want out, you have it, ole buddy. Right now! I'd like to see just how well you stand on your own two feet, Ben. With no Knievel to sell. Yeah, it would be rightly interesting."

Ben Andrews seemed to transmute right before Knievel's eyes. Instead of a man bent and determined, sure of himself, indignant at so-called wrongs, Andrews became a sniveling, wheedling, cringing toady. "Gee, Evel, who said I wanted out? No way. I don't want out. Hey look, Evel, we've got a jump coming up here. We're all set. We're ready as we've ever been. I got no complaints, Evel."

Knievel came up off the bed and stood before Ben as if to size up his sincerity. Andrews raised his right hand as if taking a pledge. Boy Scout's honor. Hand on the Bible. "I swear, Evel, I'm a happy fella. One really happy dude. I swear it. I'm happy."

Knievel straightened up the golf bag and began to slide the clubs back inside. "All right, happy man. Make me happy."

"Sure, Evel, sure. You'll get your share."

"That's all I want. Just my share. No pay . . . no Evel. Got that?"

"Sure, all you have to do is ask. That's all. Just ask."

But Knievel didn't ask—he simply extended a flattened palm that was in need of being covered.

Reluctantly, Ben extracted a thick wad of bills from his pocket and peeled off a few fifties. Knievel's frown refused to go away. "It wasn't a sell-out, you know," Ben fudged. Knievel kept on frowning. More fifties were peeled off and placed vertically across Knievel's palm.

"Thank you, Ben. Now don't let me catch you pulling this cheap stuff again. You got that?"

"I've got it, Evel, I've got it loud and clear."

"Now get the hell out, Ben. The air stinks in here. I need to clear it."

"Sure, Evel, sure." Ben wasted no time in clearing out.

Knievel couldn't resist chuckling to himself. It was a good thing his mother had warned him about men like Ben Andrews.

6

Conspiracy

THE Stanley Millard estate, one of several homes lining Millionaire's Row in Beverly Hills, was an imposing chateau in imitation of the style of Louis XIV, its tall iron gates and surrounding stone walls blatantly espousing an exclusivity common to the area.

Its architecture, inspired by Jules Mansart, included ocher-colored stone, glazed roof tiles, white shutters and a sunny terrace surfaced with polished flat stones and bejeweled by plants of numerous varieties.

Sloping from that terrace were a series of rambling gardens, less carefully prepared than the grounds immediately surrounding the mansion, but colorful nevertheless with beds of orange lilies, French marigolds, chrysanthemums and madonna lilies.

There any pretension of classiness stopped, for Stanley Millard was not entirely a classy man.

The swimming pool was early Johnny Weissmuller. The pool bar was strictly Errol Flynn circa 1935, consisting of a flat mahogany base and two oak shelves beneath for bottles. It was protected from the sun by an orange canopy in the shape of a half-tent. Mainly it was there to protect the eyes of the bartender, for Millard was emphatic about just the right amount of vermouth in his martinis.

As a matter of fact, Millard had no class at all. If the wrong amount of gin or vermouth was discovered in his martini, he was not above shouting vehemently at the hapless bartender. Bartenders, in fact, had been known to be fired for less.

On the surface, Millard was a distinguished man in his mid forties, with a shock of prematurely white hair that succeeded in making him that much more urbane, attractive and polished. His dress was impeccable, his fingernails well cleaned and trimmed. He was a stylish and discreet man because he had devoted his life to being stylish and discreet.

For good reason.

Stanley Millard was one of the most successful drug pushers in Southern California. It was a case of clean fingernails but dirty hands.

He, however, did not think of himself as a prosperous drug pusher with dirty hands. He thought of himself as a clever promoter of sporting events—a sideline he had begun as an idle venture and then parlayed into a highly profitable enterprise which his colossal ego would not permit him to drop.

He also thought of himself as a leader, a man who did not *ever* work for someone else. Only for himself, only for his own personal gain. It was true he was part of the Organization, but he thought of himself as *being* the Organization, and not just a small part of it.

He was a Jay Gatsby, perhaps less articulate than his literary counterpart in intellectual conversations, but a Gatsby in the sense that he was always seeking approval and equal footing with the *crème de la crème*, rubbing elbows with the elite, hobnobbing with Hollywood stars.

Millard was an ambitious man with exorbitant tastes and he believed that in order to satisfy those ambitions he needed large sums of cash. With abundant cash he knew he could buy anything (or anyone) he wanted—including social acceptance. He had found that acceptance here in Beverly Hills. He found it even in the face of the bartender when his martini was served near the side of the pool.

But Millard had a problem. No matter how much money he could "earn," it was never enough. This was the motivating force behind his existence: to make more money. And this morning he felt especially motivated.

Millard sprawled in a chaise longue beside the Johnny Weissmuller swimming pool, reading the *Los Angeles Times'* sporting section. He smiled only slightly as he turned to face Gunther Cortland, his attorney.

Cortland was older than Millard—he was well past fifty and his dress was less than impeccable. He had a haggard, drawn face—deep furrows across his forehead, sagging cheek muscles, flabby earlobes, and eyes that reflected fatigue, and perhaps a touch of fear. A pencil-thin moustache was his only oleaginous characteristic.

Cortland's hands were just as filthy as Millard's after many years of fronting for the Organization, the main difference being that his fingernails were actually dirty. He had never undergone a manicure in his life.

Since Cortland was less meticulous than Millard, he was less prone to good fortune. The Organization had been good to Cortland, but not as good as it might have been.

He had made mistakes in the Organization—not the kind for which one had to forfeit one's life, but big enough to stall his advancement.

All his life Cortland had clawed desperately for a shot at the main chance. He was shrewd but he was also gullible—another weakness for which he had paid over the years by being handed the chaff instead of the wheat.

But now Cortland thought only of the main chance, and he sensed that the first step toward that opportunity could be taken when Millard walked to the bar to speak to the man standing there.

That man was Jessie Hammond. Scars crisscrossed his youthful face, reminders of his dangerous way of life: racing sports cars, dune buggies, motorcycles . . . and now jumping. Yet those scars didn't detract from his rugged good looks. He had an infectious smile enhanced by pearly white teeth and a bushy head of light blond hair. In short, he was a crowd pleaser and decidedly a ladies' man. Groupies had been known to come from several states whenever his name appeared on a stadium banner.

Hammond was tense and moody, a coiled spring of a man with an obvious chip on his shoulder, strutting through life like a proud, horny bull.

He was a young man in a hurry, who wanted all that life had to offer by tomorrow afternoon. And if he didn't have it by then, heaven help the man who stood in his way.

He had twenty-twenty vision, and yet he was blind. He failed to see those who had as much as, or less than, he, only those who had more. He had courage and he wasn't afraid to face the most death-defying situations, and yet he was jealous of Knievel, for subconsciously he knew that the stuntman had something special he didn't have—something Jessie had spent a lot of time searching for but never finding.

Millard folded the *Times*, rose from the chaise longue and walked to the bar. Jessie poured himself another drink.

"I see by the papers that your friend Evel Knievel has just made a deal for another record-breaking jump for another record-breaking price . . . he's getting eighty-five thousand dollars for this one."

Despite the anger Jessie felt deep within him, he sounded envious when he replied, "Yeah, I saw the paper, Mr. Millard." The chip was back on his shoulder, and the defiance that was so habitual with him returned when he added, "You're supposed to be the number one sports promoter in the world. Top that!"

"I can top it. But I'll need your help," said Millard, sipping his martini indifferently.

Jessie crossed to Millard, staring him in the eye. "Me the number one?"

"I'll make you the top bike jumper in this country, if not the world."

"That almost sounds like a promise, Mr. Millard."

"I'm not in the habit of idle chatter, Jessie."

"You aren't kidding . . ."

"You bet your sweet ass I'm not."

Millard took Jessie by the arm and led him toward the mansion. "That's a contract. You start tonight. We go from there."

Jessie was confident as he said, "It's as good as done."

They shook hands, sealing their agreement. Afterwards, Millard wiped the palm of his hand on his dressing gown, watching Jessie climb the steps to the terrace. He rejoined Cortland at poolside.

"I think he's got guts," said Cortland. "His jumps prove that."

"Yes," agreed Millard, "but he'll never be the star Knievel is. He's missing something. Flair, charisma, gallantry. Those are the characteristics that elude Jessie . . . and he knows it . . . and it eats away at him."

"And it forces him right into our hands."

"Yes, well," said Millard, rubbing his hands together, "one takes all the advantages offered one . . . doesn't one."

"Does Jessie know anything about our plans?" asked Cortland.

"He knows *his* part of the plan . . . helping us get Knievel down into Mexico."

Cortland was visibly distressed; his voice climbed. "I'm still against using Jessie to make our deal with Knievel. He double-crossed Evel once. I think Knievel'll kick his butt straight out of the arena."

Millard disagreed. "If it were any other man but Knievel, I'd say maybe you're right, Gunther. But I've studied that big bastard. He's a man who holds no grudges. With him it's always forgive and forget. Jessie was a friend once, he'll be a friend again."

"I hope you're right, Stanley. We've got a lot riding on this."

"More than a lot. Everything." Millard stood up to greet a sandy-haired, blue-eyed, slightly built man in a wrinkled gabardine suit.

Norman Clark said good morning and handed over a large manila envelope. Millard removed several eight by ten glossy blow-ups.

"This is everything I shot yesterday," explained Clark.

The top photograph was of Knievel's Harley-Davidsons lined up outside the stadium with Will Atkins tinkering on them. "What about these bikes?" Millard asked.

Clark shrugged. "Basically they're standard Harleys. There're some minor gearing changes. Nothing that we can't tune in on pretty quick."

The next few photographs were of the equipment rig. "Only exteriors?" asked Millard.

Clark nodded.

"We'll have to work on that," suggested Millard. "Now, what can you tell us about the rig?"

"There's a lot to tell. Nothing standard about this at all. The only one of its kind in the world. Gold-leaf lettering. Custom doors and windows. Special wheel covers. The interior, that's the hitch. A match-up is going to be a major job."

Millard was the epitome of confidence. "Nothing that can't be done, if you want to do it badly enough. I believe those are the words of Mr. Knievel himself. Gunther, what's our total investment to date?"

Cortland thought for only a moment, mentally running numbers through his head. "Our investment is simple: fifty thousand, give or take a few dollars. The big money is paying for the merchandise." He paused, almost afraid to state the figure. Then: "Three million six hundred thousand dollars."

It was awhile before Millard answered. "Jesus, it's high. All right, I spent more than I figured . . . so I'll make more than I figured. Now, what about the rig?"

"It should be here sometime today," said Cortland. "Barton is wheeling."

"What can we expect?"

"Exteriorwise, the rig will be identical to Knievel's in

every respect of size. It'll have a dull finish—a primer gray, like the first coat of paint applied to all bare metal of cars and trucks before the paint is applied."

"Then the finishing touches to the van," said Clark.

"And then the finishing touches to Mr. Evel Knievel," said Millard.

7.

Nightmare

THE S.S. Knievel was secure for the night. A light burned in the recreational rig, where Knievel was going over contracts for upcoming jumps.

In the equipment van, a wooden ramp led from the trailer to the ground. Will Atkins was in the repair-shop area, alone, working on one of the Harleys on which Knievel normally performed his warm-up wheelies. His tools were scattered carelessly around him; the treasure chest was beside him, its lid temptingly open.

Knievel knew about the bottle of Bourbon De Luxe and Will knew that he knew—it was one of those strange games men tend to play when they respect each other and don't want to shatter the normalcy of the other's world.

Will fought the urge to glance at the treasure chest, but finally succumbed. He took a stiff belt of bourbon, and was putting the bottle away when he was aware of someone standing at the head of the wooden ramp.

Jessie Hammond was in snappy spirits, warm in his greeting to Will, but Will looked at him as though he were a stray dog. Will resumed working, as if Jessie didn't exist. Jessie came inside anyway, pretending to admire the equipment.

Jessie spoke first. "Guess neither of us has changed. I figured I'd find you up and working. Even at this hour."

Will dropped his wrench to the floor. "It's my job."

"Yeah, I know. Evel depends on you. I used to work here, remember?"

Will came erect and looked straight at Jessie. "That's something you wouldn't know anything about. Dependability."

Jessie shrugged off the indictment—he had a back like a duck's. "You referring to that time Evel and I were touring and I split?"

"The word is quit." Will continued to work on the broken chain, dropping each tool carelessly as if he intended the clattering noises to irritate Jessie.

"Ah, come on, Will. I was new then. A greenhorn. I didn't know anything. Just starting out. Then I got a better offer. Besides, all that was a long time ago."

"I remember it like yesterday."

"Hey then," said Jessie jubilantly, "let's drink to tomorrow, Will. What do you say? Hey, I bet you keep it in the same old place." Jessie went directly to the treasure chest and lifted the wooden lid. Will watched contemptuously as he brought out the bottle of Bourbon De Luxe.

Will snorted. "You ever think of buying a bottle?"

"If I did," replied Jessie, raising the bottle to his lips, "what would you have to bitch at me about?"

"I'd think of something," said Will, turning his back on Jessie, returning to the Harley's broken chain. Once again tools clattered.

Jessie glanced over his shoulder at Will, satisfied that the mechanic was absorbed in his work. Turning toward the door so his back was to Will, Jessie dropped a tiny capsule into the bottle. He shook the contents, replaced the cap on the bottle and walked back to the wooden chest. "Hey, that sure did hit the spot."

Will growled, "Gimme that bottle."

"Sure, pal, here you go."

Will tilted his head back and drank deeply.

"Where's Evel?" asked Jessie, trying to make his remark sound like small talk.

Will finished his swallow, wiped his mouth with the back of his greasy hand and replaced the cap on the bourbon bottle. "Just follow the crowd, junior," he told Jessie.

Jessie walked toward the rampway. "Yeah, well, thanks for the advice, old-timer."

Jessie was gone before Will realized it. He lowered himself to the rear wheel of the Harley and picked up his wrench. He angled to face the chain sprocket.

And dropped the wrench.

The chain sprocket had shifted into the rear foot peg—they had become one and the same.

Will closed his eyes and shook his head. He became aware of a whirring noise. His tongue felt as though it were sticking to the roof of his mouth.

He opened his eyes to see that the gearshift pedal was rushing up to meet the transmission; the throttle grip was becoming part of the ignition switch, and the saddle was falling down into the area of the rear foot peg, which was still linked to the chain sprocket. "Oh my God . . ."

The interior of the van shouldn't have been spinning—not after only a couple of snorts. And small snorts at that. Was he reaching the point where he couldn't take it any longer? Was this what they called the DT's? He rubbed his eyes. Bats coming out of the wall . . . would he be seeing those next?

The Harley got worse. The front brake had drifted up onto the instrument panel, the instrument panel into the clutch lever, the clutch lever into the throttle grip.

It wasn't a Harley any more. It was a mazework of machinery, all twisted and distorted and misaligned. The result of a crazed brain. *My* brain, Will told himself; a sober man doesn't look at a Harley and see a mechanical nightmare.

Will, I need you.

He knew the voice, but he didn't want to acknowledge that he knew it.

Linda.

Will, I need you.

He didn't have to see her to know where she was. It was the hospital room. The one he should have been in that day she gave birth to Tommy. The day he'd cracked into—

Where are you when I need you, Will?

He concentrated on the motorcycle. The Harley was moving now—drifting into air. First three feet to the right, then three feet to the left. Up three feet, down three feet. Air cleaner into rear shock absorbers.

I'm right here, Linda. I'm here in the room with you.

I can't see you, Will. I can't see you.

Hold out your hand, Linda.

I can't find your hand, Will. God, Will, I think I'm going to die. The baby is too much for me, Will.

Where's the doctor? There should be a doctor.

The doctor can't help me, Will. Only you can do that. Please come to me, Will.

I want to, Linda, but I have to do the jump. You do understand, honey. I have to—

"Hold onto those handlebars, Will. I adjusted them just the way you like them."

"Eddie, you sure on the distance?"

"Eighty feet, tiger. You'll do it as easy as butter spreads

on rye. Just remember to power in and glide out. And don't forget, Will, I couldn't convince the promoter to salt the snakes. Those rattlers are poisonous as well."

Will, don't leave me.

"It's not the snakes, Eddie. I don't like that wet grass."

Will, don't ever leave me, please.

He realized, in a moment of lucidity, that he was lying on the floor of the van. He couldn't remember falling, only that he was sprawled there like some skid row drunkard. He tried to raise his head. He couldn't. It felt like a thousand-pound weight.

Click! There was a brilliant flash of light above him. He felt its warmth and it made him feel secure.

In another blinding moment of lucidity he realized he wasn't on the floor after all. No, hell no, he was on the Spanish bike. He felt the pressure of the saddle on his buttocks; he felt the weight of his legs pressed down hard on the foot pegs. He was gunning the engine of the Cappra 250-MX and he was streaking along the football field, sliding on the wet grass.

The take-off ramp loomed ahead. What had Eddie said about the rattlers?

They were poisonous.

Hell, he wasn't worried about the snakes, anyway. They were between the ramps, only there to bother him should he come down short.

No way that he, Will Atkins, the greatest bike jumper in the world, was going to come down short.

The Cappra 250-MX was moving faster now, the take-off ramp coming up fast. Then he was sliding. Sliding in the wet grass.

Will, the baby, it's—

He'd warned Eddie about the wet grass. He couldn't hold the Cappra steady; he wasn't going to hit the center of the ramp. He was crooked and he knew it and he tried to cut his speed to abort the jump.

It was too late. He was on the ramp, angled off to the left. He tried to rectify, even though he knew it was too late, and he tried to re-accelerate to build up the speed he would need to complete the jump successfully.

Click! Another circle of light above him, blinding him. Was he on the floor or was he on the bike?

The bike! The Cappra drifted lazily above the pit of

snakes, sailing without enough power to reach the landing ramp.

The rattlers! Eddie had warned him about the rattlers being the real thing.

Venom.

He didn't hear anything. He didn't hear the crowd, he didn't hear the rush of wind past his face, he didn't hear the roar of the Cappra.

All he could hear was the sound of rattlers. Shaking their tails by the dozens. By the hundreds. By the thousands. His brain was crawling with fear.

The Cappra began the descent of its trajectory. God, he was falling right into the middle of the rattlers. Thank God they were caged up in crates.

Front wheel. Incredible impact.

Click! There was that strange blast of light again.

Linda!

He was floating through space. He felt air. He heard hissing. He felt several things. The moisture of grass. A pain in his back.

A crashing. The bike! Roll to avoid the bike. Too late. The bike skidded past him, flattening the grass of the football field.

He heard breaking wood. He heard the rattlers again. Something had invaded their domicile and they were angry.

He wanted to run. He felt the pain in his back again. Sharply. He couldn't move. He wanted to move only an inch, but not even that was allowed by the pain in his back. Something wriggled across the leg of his jumpsuit. He knew what it was but he refused to look. Something else crawled across the top of his stomach. It paused, then continued on.

He looked above him and thought he saw the face of one of the mechanics. Was it Eddie? Or an ambulance attendant? Jessie Hammond.

What the hell was Jessie Hammond doing here?

"Hey, Jess, help me out of this goddamn snake pit."

Click. Another circle of light. The sun? The moon? That couldn't be. He was on the floor of the van.

No, he was on the football field. Listen to that cheering crowd.

Pop! His brain was illuminated for a fraction of a second.

Your spine's broken, Will.

End of your career, Will. Your jumping days are done.

He saw the face clearly now. Hell yes, that was Jessie

53

Hammond standing over him. Was that a camera in his hands? Christ, Jessie, quit taking pictures and help me up.

He froze. A rattler was crawling across his stomach, angling its head toward his face. He saw them all now: the ambulance attendants, the doctor, the spectators, Eddie. And Jessie Hammond. They were all watching the snake and laughing their heads off.

The snake's head was resting on Will's neck. Its tongue darted out, touching his chin.

He didn't dare move.

"You can get up now."

"Sure, Will, go ahead and get up."

The rattler was coiling.

And striking.

Linda! Save me, Linda. Nobody else will save me!

You should have been here, Will. Now it's too late. I can't help you either, Will.

Click!

The last thing he remembered was Jessie Hammond picking up the rattler and bringing it down next to his face, close enough for the fangs to sink into his flesh.

He screamed and then there was nothing.

"Come on out of it, old boy. Come on, Will, time to rise and shine."

The first thing Will saw was Knievel's face peering down into his. He sat up with a start, brushing some invisible thing off his chest. The frantic look left his eyes and he leaned against the wall of the van for support. His brain, and his body, felt hopelessly numb.

The trailer doors were still wide open, just as he had left them the night before. The wooden ramp was also still in position. Despite the brilliant sunlight, the interior lights were burning. Just as he had left them.

"A bad night, Will? You oughta try a bed sometime. Does wonders for your back."

"The bikes are ready," said Will, as if that might alleviate Knievel's anger.

"How about you? You gotta lay off the sauce, Will. You're trying to destroy yourself."

"Sauce? I only had a couple."

"Yeah, sure." Knievel picked up the bottle of Bourbon De Luxe. He turned it upside down to remind Will it was a dead soldier. "Here's your proof."

ssional level, but with Jessie that came hard. Especially case of Evel Knievel.

ssie was jarred from his reverie by the roar of a Harley. ooked up to see Knievel on the north edge of the playing , revving his motorcycle, each burst like a word that lenged Jessie.

nd it was a form of challenge. For Knievel then placed helmet squarely on his head, tapped it firmly into place came straight at Jessie. Moving at sixty miles an hour. d giving no indication that he intended to swerve to avoid llision.

Jessie remained unruffled on the outside, but inside he as in utter turmoil. He watched the bike moving toward im and realized, as only a biker could, that Knievel was laying a game with him.

Chicken on Two Wheels.

And there was no doubt in Jessie's mind that Knievel expected him to play the game, not turn tail and skedaddle. It was Knievel's way, Jessie knew, of checking to see if he still had his gumption; to see if somewhere along the way in the past few years he had lost his nerve. It was a challenge of his manhood, a test of his fortitude.

Jessie tightened up but stood fast. If there was any single game a biker feared most, it was Chicken on Two Wheels.

Jessie remembered an earlier Chicken game, in Barstow, California, in March 1966, when he had been part of "Evel Knievel and the Motorcycle Daredevils." Knievel had stood in the center of the field while a three-hundred-sixty-pound Harley bore down on him, moving at sixty-five miles an hour.

It was intended that he jump high enough for the bike to pass beneath him, but it hadn't worked out that way. The cycle had struck him squarely in the groin and thighs after he had jumped only a foot and a half off the ground.

Knievel had gone into the air fifteen feet, turned two somersaults in mid air and landed with a crunch on his back. A highway patrolman covered him with a blanket, assuming that no one could have survived such impact. But he wasn't dead. He was paralyzed. His ribs were cracked and broken. He was sprained from the bottom of his feet clear up to his waist. He spent more than a month in the hospital. But he wasn't dead.

And now Jessie was the one standing in the middle of a playing field, with a machine hurtling toward him, unstop-

Knievel suddenly exploded into motion, throwing the empty bottle at the trailer wall as hard as he could.

"I don't like people committing suicide around me."

Knievel took the handlebars of one of the Harleys and wheeled it to the edge of the ramp. He gave Will one final glance, then rolled the bike to the ground.

Will was still dazed, still trying to get his bearings. What the hell had happened here last night?

Slowly, painfully, he moved to the switch, shutting down the lights. "Doesn't make sense," he muttered, but there was no one left to listen to him.

8.

Hairy Ride

JESSIE Hammond, looking cool and casual in
hand-embroidered cowboy shirt, Levi's and bl
boots, stood in the center of the Long Beach
Memorial Stadium.

He noted it was a functional, if not beauteous, s
arena with two sets of grandstands. The main secti
reinforced concrete on pile foundation, had a seating
ity of 12,500, its seats constructed of yellow Alaskan
There were seven entrance ramps. A smaller set of bleac
known as the East Grandstand, seated 2000.

The athletic field was about 310 feet wide and 870
long, with an eight-foot masonry wall extending north a
south from the grandstands across the ends of the athlet
field. The track was 33 feet wide and had ten running lane
A 220-yard straightaway in front of the West Grandstand
continued on to form a 440-yard oval with another 220-yard
straightaway on the east side of the field.

Jessie sized up the field and decided Knievel had chosen
his jump site intelligently. Ample room for the takeoff and
landing ramps, plus whatever he intended to place between
them. Knievel's career had reached the point, Jessie realized,
that leaping over a row of automobiles was no longer spectacular enough. Knievel had to top himself each time, and
that meant a new gimmick more exciting than the last. Not
even thirteen double-decker buses had made that much of
an impression on the slightly-jaded fans at Wembley. After
the success of *Jaws,* Knievel had vowed to take a death-
defying leap over an open cage of man-eating sharks, but
had yet to try it.

Whatever Knievel chose, Jessie knew it would be spectacular, and he experienced a twinge of jealousy, of envy,
of unmitigated hatred. He tried to keep such feelings on a

57

pable. Sure, he could move a step to the right or the left and Knievel would break it off right now. But where would that leave him? If there was anyone he had to get on the good side of right now, it was Knievel. So Jessie held his ground. He would show them he had the chutzpah—just like Knievel—to face a hurtling three-hundred-sixty-pound Harley.

The distance was closing fast. Jessie would have to coordinate the jump with the speed of the bike. Best way was to count . . . one two three four Jesus Christ here it comes five six seven—

Long before the bike reached him, Jessie leaped high into the air, throwing out his left leg as far as possible to form a wide inverted V which started at his crotch and ran to both jumpboots. No sooner was he in the air than Knievel was shooting beneath him, the helmet barely grazing Jessie's thighs.

Jessie came down squarely on both feet; as he landed he felt a surge of power. He, not Knievel, was the King of the Jumpers. Not even Knievel had been able to pull off that stunt back in '66.

Knievel turned the Harley and rode back to a stop beside Jessie. "Figured you'd remember that stunt I tried to pull off in Barstow when we were workin' together. Figured you wouldn't make the same mistake I did and end up in a hospital. Figured you'd know exactly what to do. Seeing as how I trained you."

Jessie was feeling cocky as hell, and Knievel's compliment almost shot him into the stratosphere. With Millard backing his play, he was going to be number one Jumper. *Numero uno.* Hot damn!

"Hey, Jessie, what the hell you doin' round here? Last I heard, you were sticking your neck out down around Florida. Swamp jumping?"

"Kid stuff. Chicken feed, Evel. I'm tied into something better. Which is what I want to talk to you about."

In a Cadillac convertible as pure white as the soap she had once sold in TV commercials, Kate Morgan drove onto the stadium playing field, conspicuously jerking to a stop with a squeal of her brakes.

Jessie could sense he was quickly losing Knievel's attention as he saw a beautiful woman stretch her pantherlike body, get out of the convertible and walk around to its trunk.

"I'll see you later, Jessie," said Knievel. "Right now I've got some business to attend to."

"I can see what kind of business," said Jessie good-naturedly.

Knievel kicked the engine of the Harley back to life and raced away, as if the convertible (or its occupant) had some magnetic pull on him.

Business. Jessie snorted. He'd show Knievel the business, all right.

Kate had just removed her camera bag from the trunk when Knievel pulled alongside. "Hi," he said casually, as though he had just been passing through the neighborhood. She nodded politely, barely acknowledging Knievel's presence.

"What're you doing out here today, Kate?"

"Messing around."

Well, at least she answered. That was something. Knievel straddled his weight on the bike as he said, "Look, since you're doing a 'cycle story you ought to know what you're talking about. Ever been on one of these?"

Kate shook her head. Knievel might have been a leaf being blown across the field by a wind for all the attention she was giving him.

"Let's go for a ride, then."

"No thank you," she said, looking more at the grandstands than at Knievel. "I've got some equipment to check out today."

Despite the frustration that was rising in him, Knievel was once again struck by Kate's beauty. She wore no makeup and her hair cascaded around her shoulders, producing a soft effect. She was again stylishly dressed: beige knee-length skirt, green blouse, red scarf.

Kate unzipped her gadget bag. The sound seemed to serve as a punctuation to her refusal.

"You're chicken, huh?"

For the first time that morning, Kate looked fully at Knievel. Well, he thought, forbidding himself the pleasure of a smile, I finally got to her. How about that.

Kate didn't reply. She simply placed her gadget bag in the front seat of the convertible, adjusted the scarf around her neck, and climbed onto the back of the motorcycle as though she had done it a hundred times before.

It was a ride he wanted her to remember. Something that

would imprint a lasting impression on her thoughts, so that when she wrote about what it was like to be on a bike with Evel Knievel, she would have something solid and authentic to tell her readers.

As she placed her warm hands against his sides, he sensed in Kate a relaxation, an inner calmness and imperturbability unusual in someone who was riding for the first time. Such sangfroid was not only rare in a woman but refreshing.

As Knievel began to perform wheelies, following the curvature of the oval track, her grasp on him never tightened, but remained uniformly gentle.

He decided it was a form of self-collectedness that Kate had developed during her foreign assignments covering tense political situations and South American coups d'état. The best reaction in fear-riddled situations like those was to show no fear. It set you apart from the predicament, kept you from becoming part of it. The result was level-headed objectivity and seeming indifference or aplomb. She might also have developed this fearlessness, he decided, during her mountain-climbing and shark-hunting expeditions.

Knievel performed two more laps around the track, aloft in the wheelie position all the time, then shot through Number Three Exit and out into the vacant parking lot.

He took from the machine all the power it could muster so that Kate would feel the sensation of the wind against her face, feel the vibration against her legs and buttocks, have her thoughts battered senseless by the roar of the engine.

Knievel wanted those thoughts battered senseless so that after a few minutes she would no longer feel the wind or sense the vibration or hear the noise. Once those superficialities of bike riding had canceled themselves out, she would feel the tranquillity and the insouciance that comes from lengthy riding; she would begin to experience the *true* sensation of motorcycling.

To Knievel, that was a state of mind in which the responsibilities of the workaday world and the accompanying worries and headaches could be displaced and forgotten. It was an emotion of isolation, but it was a positive form of isolation. It was the isolation of one's mind that enabled a crystal-like lucidity that in turn could lead to new thoughts, new emotions.

Knievel kept circling the parking lot, hoping Kate was perceiving some sense of rapture. He returned to the field via

Number Four Exit Ramp and angled immediately into the main grandstand, climbing the central stairs in the hope that Kate's hands would tighten their grip on his sides. But they didn't—she remained unfazed by the bumping, jarring motion of the bike. In a fit of frustration, Knievel swung the bike around and returned to the field to perform more wheelies. He seesawed the bike erratically, at one point feigning loss of control—again to evoke some response from Kate.

Knievel realized he was wasting his time, and gasoline, so he slowed the bike, pulling up beside the convertible.

Kate dismounted, again like a professional rider, and unknotted her red scarf. She reached for the gadget bag as though nothing had happened. As though she were back to the moment when Knievel had first driven up to her to propose the challenge. "That was sweet," she said tonelessly, adjusting the lens of her Nikon.

"Sweet?" His voice was pierced by incredulity.

"I suppose," she said coolly, "that the exciting part is the jump." She walked toward the stadium, checking through the Nikon's viewfinder, looking for camera angles.

Knievel removed his crash helmet, scratched his head and refused to take his eyes off her swaying body. It was only after she had disappeared into one of the stadium tunnels that he threw the helmet to the ground in frustration.

It was the first time he could remember that a woman had walked so casually around the ego of Evel Knievel.

9.

Homecoming

TOMMY Atkins was ten years and four days old.
He carried a battered brown leather suitcase in one hand,
a large dog-eared scrapbook in the other.

He wore penny loafers, gray flannels, a blazer with in-
signia and a shirt with a button-down collar and tie. He was
a walking model for a prep school.

And he looked like the happiest kid in the world.

Not that Tommy Atkins had a great deal to be happy
about. He had never known his mother and he had never
seen his father.

Shunted from an indifferent aunt and uncle to a boarding
school, he had somehow found the strength to face up to
life. He had never allowed a feeling of defeat to totally win
over him.

If life had robbed him of his youth, Tommy Atkins had
never complained about it. It was too late to start now. At the
age of ten, he was a very old young man.

Tommy felt a lump in his throat as he crossed the parking
lot of the Long Beach stadium and headed toward the
Knievel vehicles.

He saw a man working on a Harley-Davidson beside the
equipment van, and he felt a surge of excitement within him.
The man turned to pick up a cup of coffee, put it to his lips
. . . but froze when he saw the boy walking toward him.

Tommy approached the man slowly, studying his face.
The man flung away his coffee cup and lurched up the rampway into the equipment van. Tommy stood motionless for a
moment, not knowing exactly what he should do. Again, he
refused to let disappointment curtail the feeling of initial
excitement he had felt and he climbed the rampway.

Inside, he found the man standing next to a tool bench,
holding an old photograph in his greasy hands. There was

63

no mistaking who the man was. Tommy had never seen him in person before, but he had studied his photographs often enough.

"Dad?"

Will Atkins' reaction was one of belligerent annoyance as he turned to face the son he had never faced before. Will dropped the photograph into a drawer and slammed it shut.

"I'm Tommy."

Will was silent. He was over the initial shock now, and he was left with the blind anger and resentment he had always felt toward his son.

"Tommy," the boy repeated. "Your son."

Will stepped forward and towered above the slight figure of the boy. He spoke without a trace of sentiment, as he might speak to a passing stranger, or a panhandler. "Yeah, I know who you are. Where the hell did you come from?" He didn't speak the words—he growled them.

Tommy placed his suitcase on the floor next to one of the motorcycles, keeping the scrapbook under one armpit as though it were his most valuable possession, no matter how dog-eared it looked. "I'm through with school. I graduated."

Will snorted contemptuously. "Graduated? From what? Kindergarten? What the hell do you mean, you graduated?"

Tommy managed a weak smile. "Our school only goes through the sixth grade. I'm ready for junior high now."

"You still didn't answer my question," Will accused harshly. "What the hell're you doing here?" He gestured wildly with his arms. "Don't you go to summer camp or something?"

For the first time, Tommy permitted a note of defeat to tinge his voice. "The school wrote you asking about this summer, sir . . . but . . . but you didn't answer their letters."

Will's reply was almost lost under his breath. "I'm moving around all the time. Sometimes letters get lost. The post office is always fouled up. So maybe I didn't get any letter, okay?"

Tommy shifted the scrapbook to his left hand and extended his right in a gesture of warmth. "I'm glad to meet you."

Will shoved his greasy hands out in front of him, showing the palms to Tommy. "You'll just get them all messed up. You know, I work for a living."

Tommy didn't pull in his hand. He waited patiently. "Please . . ."

64

Finally Will wiped his hands on his coveralls and shook hands with Tommy. He pulled his hand back as though the boy personified an infectious disease. There was no way for Tommy to conceal his nervousness—he continued to shift the scrapbook from hand to hand, armpit to armpit.

Truculently, Will said, "You're not going to like it around here. No breakfast in bed."

"We make our own beds in school," said the boy defensively, weary of taking a beating and ready now to get his back up if he had to.

Will frowned as he noticed Tommy shifting the scrapbook. "What the hell's that you're handling like a hot potato?"

"Newspaper write-ups," replied Tommy, beaming. He couldn't restrain the pride he felt. "A lot of clippings . . . I guess you could call it a scrapbook."

"Evel'll like that. He enjoys reading about himself."

"These aren't about Evel. They're about *you*."

There was a quiet kind of triumph in the way Tommy opened the scrapbook—treating it like something sacred. "Here's where you jumped in New York."

"I'll be damned," mused Will.

"And here's where you were first in the Texas championship."

Will took the scrapbook gently from Tommy and flipped through it slowly, stony-faced. "Hey, look at this," he said, his voice climbing. " 'Will Atkins Jumps Lizard Canyon.' I've never seen this clipping before."

Will kept turning the pages, becoming lost in a private reverie. Each page was covered with yellowing newspaper clippings and magazine articles. There were huge photographs of Will on his different jump cycles; in his many multicolored costumes. There were photographs of his triumphs, his defeats, his successes and his disasters. The clippings came to a sudden end and Will paused.

His career should have continued, should have filled the remainder of the scrapbook. The bitterness of it all swept over him again, and he was angry to have been reminded of it all so vividly. He stared hopelessly at the empty pages.

"I've been collecting things about you all my life, sir," said Tommy softly, removing the scrapbook from Will's hands. He placed it under his arm again.

Will pushed his cap back on his head, shaking himself loose from the unpleasant memories. "Forget it," he said, his voice suddenly hoarse, his throat parched dry. "Like I have.

It's ancient history." He said it almost accusingly, as if it might have been Tommy's fault that his career had suddenly stopped.

"It's not old to me," countered Tommy. "It's like yesterday."

"Forget that yesterday crap," shouted Will, yanking the scrapbook from Tommy's grasp and flinging it toward the open doors. It struck the greasy floor and slid against the treasure chest.

Tommy's mouth hung open, as if he had been struck across the face by Will's fist. He looked from the scrapbook back to Will, waiting for some explanation, some understanding of why he had done such an outrageous thing. Tommy looked hard at Will, and a thousand daydreams were exploded in an instant by the hateful look on his father's face.

There was no time for Will to say anything. Knievel and his Harley came up the rampway behind Tommy. Knievel leaped from the bike and flung his arms around the boy. "You gotta be Tommy," cried Knievel. "I recognize you from your picture. Hey, I'm sure glad to see you. Welcome aboard the S.S. Knievel. You're a full-fledged deckhand now."

"H—hello, Mr. Knievel. Sure glad to meet you." The exuberance and warmth of Knievel had, for the moment, alleviated the bitterness he had felt toward his father. It was an antidote to the tears that had begun to form in Tommy's eyes.

"Knock off that 'mister' business, old buddy. 'Evel' to you. Hey, what a great surprise. Your dad never even told me you were coming. Come on, Will, let's take a break and show Tommy around. Let him get used to the setup. He's gonna be part of the entourage for a while."

"No thanks, Evel, I've got work to do on the bikes." Will's voice was still hoarse, his throat still harsh. "You two go ahead."

Knievel slid an arm around Tommy. "Tommy, your dad takes great care of these bikes for me. That helps take care of my life, too. Hey, what do you say we take a look at my van, Tommy?"

As Knievel led Tommy away from the equipment van, he glanced over his shoulder at Will, sensing the tension in the mechanic, and a certain hesitancy in the youth. Will was staring down at the floor, his hands thrust into his back pockets. Lost in deep thought. Knievel sensed that Tommy was watching him, so he clapped the boy on the back again and brought out a new smile. "I think you're gonna like the van, Tommy."

"I've liked it ever since I first read about it, Mr. Knie . . . I mean, Evel."

"That's better, now you're getting the idea of how casual we are around here. Tommy, let me tell you. I'm sure glad you're finally here. This is going to be a great summer. We're all gonna be together now. You . . . your dad . . . and old Evel."

"Together," said Tommy. But even Knievel could detect a note of uncertainty in the boy's voice.

Only after they were gone, disappeared into Knievel's living quarters, had Will moved to the wooden chest to pick up the scrapbook.

This time he avoided the back of the book and flipped pages toward the front. He found the wedding picture, second page in.

Linda was wearing a white satin wedding gown with French lace. It was the one piece of her trousseau he had never forgotten. But the faces that stared up at him were the faces of youngsters. Of total strangers. They were radiant, hopeful faces, with the expectancy of a full, rich lifetime ahead of them, but they were the faces of strangers.

Will slammed the scrapbook shut, but he placed it gently in the treasure chest, wedging it next to the Knievel T-shirts, and carefully closed the lid.

10

Knievel's Refusal

IT was not surprising on a Wednesday afternoon, when traditionally most doctors and dentists are out improving their golf averages, to find the Eight Iron Driving Range thriving with customers.

The parking lot was jammed with automotive elegance—Cadillacs, Lincoln Continentals, Jaguar XKE's, Rolls-Royces, Mercedes Benzes—as Norman Clark, still wearing the same wrinkled garbardine suit, pulled the black, freshly waxed limousine into a space near the main entrance and switched off the ignition.

He turned to glance at Millard, who sat next to him idly running his finger across the dashboard as though he were an inspector seeking some slight trace of dust—hence an uncovering of the sloppiness around him. Clark squirmed. Any sense of security around a man like Millard was a luxury he had never enjoyed. Millard thrived on neatness, even if what he left behind him was the litter of mankind.

In the back seat, Cortland and Jessie sat in silence. Cortland's face was impassive, but not Jessie's. The young jumper leaned forward expectantly, his lips parting slightly as he glanced at the briefcase resting in Cortland's lap. Jessie looked again at Millard anticipatingly, but Millard continued to exhibit no reaction. Finally, like a cat who has tired of the mouse, he snapped his fingers. "Show him," said Millard.

Cortland's body came alive, although his face remained impassive. The air was split by a sharp pair of *snaps* as he opened the briefcase. From its neat interior he removed a cellophane packet, which he passed indifferently to Jessie.

Cortland's voice was as passionless as his face was indifferent. "You know what this is."

Jessie nodded, taking the packet eagerly. "The merchandise."

"Shall we call it," said Millard, still running his finger across the dashboard, "a random sampling."

Jessie opened one end of the packet, dipped his middle finger into the white substance, and placed it against his lips, tasting. He smiled. "Some sampling. This is the real stuff. What dreams are made of."

"When this little affair is over, Jessie," said Millard, "you'll be living your own dreams. You'll be able to afford all your pleasures. Great and small. And you'll be the number one biker."

"I have no small pleasures," returned Jessie, helping himself to a second sampling. Cortland removed the packet gingerly from his fingers and returned it to the suitcase. *Snap. Snap.* So much for the merchandise.

Millard turned slightly to pass Jessie an envelope. Inside, carefully folded, were a letter and five slips—cashier's checks.

Jessie accepted the envelope, sliding it into the pocket of his blue blazer with red trimming.

"Jessie," said Millard, "go to work. You'll be a millionaire."

Jessie smiled encouragingly at Millard, as if to say they had nothing to worry about. It was in the bag.

As the door closed, Millard leaned back against the richly upholstered seat covering, sighing inaudibly.

Cortland sat stiffly in the back seat, the briefcase wet with his perspiration. "I still think you should be handling this yourself."

Millard shook his head, chuckling softly. "This way is better."

"Jessie's not quick enough for negotiations like these."

Millard's voice was still soft and relaxed as he replied, "He doesn't have to be quick. You keep forgetting, Gunther, that Knievel likes Jessie. He broke Jessie into the jumping business."

"You still think he's our best chance?"

"He's our only chance."

Millard returned his finger to the dashboard, searching for some speck of dust or lint.

Norman Clark felt his sense of insecurity returning.

The bag of golf clubs at Knievel's feet was far from ordinary. The entire set had been scientifically graduated in length, weight and shaft stiffness, and when swung produced an identical "feel." All the wood clubs were made from

70

persimmon; all the irons were chromium-plated forged steel. The set had been "measured" to fit the man, thus producing clubs of a suppleness suited to Knievel's individual swing.

Knievel, dressed in a short-sleeved Hawaiian print, white slacks and white golfing shoes, winked at Ben Andrews as he slid his number one driver out of the bag and studied the fairway. "Wanna lay any money on this?" he asked, almost mockingly.

Andrews, who was wearing his ubiquitous straw hat and a white cotton shirt ringed with perspiration stains, puffed on a long black cigar. "No way, Evel. I know a sucker bet when I see it."

Jessie Hammond waited patiently behind them as Knievel sized up the drive, placed his green ball on the tee and drove the ball one hundred and eighty yards.

Only after he slid the number one back into the custom-made bag did Knievel—his face reflecting satisfaction with the drive—turn to consider Jessie again.

Jessie asked, "How's the swing feel, Evel?"

"About as good as yours this morning with a Harley passing under your butt."

That got an obnoxious laugh out of Andrews. He nodded toward the limousine in the parking lot. "You're running with big company, Jessie. Real big."

"It's good for the image," said Jessie, smiling.

"May as well get to the point, Jessie. What's Millard up to?"

Jessie tried to sound cool and relaxed, even if inside he was all nerves and cactus needles. "Millard wants to book us for a five-date tour down in Mexico."

Knievel slid a number five mashie from the bag, sizing up the ground. "Been having trouble with my pitch-and-run shots on the green." He bent over and placed another ball on the tee. "Mexico? Hey, I've never jumped in Mexico before." He said it as though it were an afterthought.

"Yeah," said Jessie enthusiastically. "You draw a hundred thousand bucks a jump."

Knievel whistled. Ben Andrews sneered.

"Are you kidding?" The words rolled off Andrew's tongue like drops of acid. He pointed his club at Knievel. "Let me handle you down there, Evel, and I'll get us that much for the taco concessions alone."

"What's wrong, Ben? You left out the tequila stands."

"Those too if you want them."

"Ben, you and me, we aren't hooked up for life. Don't be greedy."

"Too late for a guy like me to change now."

"I do think you'd cut your mother's heart out and sell it to the highest bidder, please your bleeding heart." Knievel took a number nine niblick in hand. "Lot of loft on the face." he said. "Hit the ball right with this baby and it rises almost vertically."

Jessie removed the envelope from his blazer and held it up temptingly. "Listen, Evel, anyone can talk money. But Millard is ready to back his claim. Here's five postdated cashier's checks. One hundred thousand each." He handed the envelope to Knievel, who took it with a mocking smile.

"Every time you jump," continued Jessie, "you just go out and cash a check. It's that simple."

Knievel whistled again. "That's half a mil, Jessie boy."

"And you're holding it right in your hot little hands."

"Real nice, Jessie. That's a lot of bread, no arguing that point. Only you have a problem."

"What problem?"

Knievel was pointing the number nine at Andrews, who stood watchfully over his tee, hands on hips, looking slightly ridiculous with his white cotton shirt hanging over his belt-line. "Ben . . . he's your problem."

Andrews grinned smugly. "I've got Evel signed for two more jumps."

"Mr. Millard will make good," promised Jessie.

"Pay me off?"

"Call it whatever you like."

"If anyone does any paying off, it'll be me," said Andrews defiantly. He swung viciously at a ball, sending it far down the fairway.

Sensing a bullheaded obstacle, Jessie turned his attention back to Knievel. "Did you sign a contract with this bird?"

Knievel rested his club over his shoulder. "I *said* I'd do two jumps."

"You *said?*"

Ben frowned. "I thought you worked with Evel. Knew him. What he says he'll *do,* he *does*."

Knievel sighed, and although he was still smiling, there was a firmness, a hardness in his voice that left no room for misinterpretation. "You heard the man, Jessie. Ben's a thieving little coyote, but he'll chase a dollar halfway to the moon and back. If I stay awake twenty-four hours a day, I get my cut."

With a shrug of his shoulders, Knievel handed the envelope back to Jessie. "Sorry," he said flatly, returning his attention to the fairway and turning his back on Jessie.

"Oh," said Ben facetiously, "I'm sorry too. But that's the way the jumping business bounces."

"Well, you think about it, Evel." Jessie stalked off, obviously angered and upset at Knievel's refusal. From his point of view, it had been a crushing defeat. Millard's plan to make him number one jumper had just gone down the toilet.

Knievel swung the niblick with an incredible force. "Goddamn, look at that, Ben. Had so much backspin on it, the ball jumped backwards."

"Forget that backwards stuff," warned Ben. "In your line of work you're supposed to jump forward."

11.

Tragedy in the Afternoon

THEY were enormous specimens, measuring ten feet from their noses to the tips of their swishing tails, and they roared with characteristic displeasure. They had not been fed for at least a day and they stalked the enclosure boldly and aggressively.

Their appetite would normally tend to buffalo, zebra, deer, wild hog, peafowl and cattle, but today they were gluttonous for a new kind of food.

Evel Knievel.

Six lions in one cage; six tigers in the other—all males, all ill-tempered, all motivated by voracious appetites, stalking back and forth, their nerves irritated by the vociferousness of the anticipative crowd cramming Long Beach Veterans Memorial Stadium.

The animals treaded their roofless cages, which had been located between the two jump ramps in the center of the playing field. The sleek creatures could instinctively sense that something was going to happen, just as the thousands of men, women and children packing the grandstands were aware of the life and death struggle that was about to be enacted.

"Look at those babies move."

"If just one of those cats got out of that pen, there'd be a panic like you wouldn't believe."

"Don't like the way they keep pawin' upward like that. How high can one of those cats jump, anyway?"

"Not that high."

"Wouldn't be too sure of that. You'd be surprised what a hungry cat can do."

"That Knievel's gotta be crazy to try this stunt."

"Not crazy. Smart. Look at all the dough he's gonna make on this jump. The stands are packed."

"Twenty bucks says Knievel gets one look at those hungry lions and he chickens."

"Knievel'll do the jump, all right. Just a question of whether or not he makes it all the way to the other side."

"Knievel's never backed down yet."

"He's fulla hot wind if you want my opinion."

"We don't wanna know your opinion. Your opinion stinks. Knievel's got guts. Whatever else you want to say about him, he's got guts."

"Anybody falls into that pit, he's gonna get ripped to shreds in a matter of seconds."

"Saw a guy get eaten alive once. Not a pretty sight."

"You're full of bull."

"And the tiger was full of man. He belched twice when he finished."

"One of those cats tries to eat Knievel, he'll die of food poisoning."

"Where the hell is that jumper? He's late."

"He's always late. It's part of his style."

"Style, my ass. I've got a heavy date tonight."

"You'll keep your date."

"Just like Knievel always keeps his date."

"Someday he's gonna keep a date with destiny."

Good afternoon, ladies and gentlemen. This is Frank Gifford speaking to you directly from sunny Southern California. We're at Long Beach Veterans Memorial Stadium here near the blue Pacific to watch Evel Knievel laying his life on the line again.

Today, Evel's impossible goal is to jump for a new world's distance record. As though that isn't heroic enough, Evel has doubled the danger. He's not jumping over buses or cars today, no sir. Instead, Evel will attempt to soar over twelve ferocious man-eating lions and tigers. Animals gathered in a cage without a roof.

You and I are lucky, ladies and gentlemen. They turned away thousands of requests for tickets. It looks as though everyone in the state of California wants to see Evel jump but right now you couldn't get a grasshopper in this arena.

In the living quarters of the S.S. Knievel, there was no mistaking the admiration on Tommy Atkins' face as Knievel zipped up his leathers. Knievel had seen that expression many times before on the faces of the young. It filled him with a warmth that made all the hardships and dangers worthwhile. It filled him with the same satisfaction he had felt that night at the Charity Hills Orphanage when Sister Charity had wished him good luck.

"Hey, Tommy," said Knievel, patting him gently on the shoulder, "I think it'd be a good idea for you to be out in the pit today."

Tommy's eyes grew ever wider. "You really mean that, Evel?"

"Damn right I mean it. You have to work to earn your keep along with the rest of us. Nobody gets a free ride in this outfit. Now, get out there, young man."

Tommy raced for the door, thanking Knievel and telling Will he would see him in the pit. Will, who had stood by the sink sipping a glass of beer, his back turned to Tommy and Knievel, didn't even look at the boy or reply. After Tommy was gone, Will poured the rest of the beer down his throat in a single gulp.

Knievel turned angrily on the mechanic, unable to control his emotions any longer. "Why the hell don't you stop knocking the kid?"

"He's my kid. I'll knock him if I want to."

"Yesterday was the first time you saw him since the day he was born."

"Look, I didn't ask the kid to come here." He slammed his empty beer glass down on the counter, afraid to look Knievel squarely in the eye.

"In twenty-four hours you haven't said a decent thing about him. Or to him. What the hell kind of a father are you, anyway?"

Will was having a hard time controlling his temper, and now he did look Knievel in the eye without faltering. "Why don't you just butt out of my life?"

Knievel pounded the edge of the counter with his fist. "You think that'll make Tommy disappear out of *your* life? Man, when I saw that kid yesterday, I really believed it was gonna be a whole new ballgame."

Will swore. "Ballgame! Everything's a sport with you, isn't it, Evel. Just one continuous jump." Will clumsily picked up his beer glass and went to the draught spigot. The beer spilled jerkily into the glass as he erratically jerked the tap. Foam dripped over the edge of the glass.

"That's better than one continuous drink or Bourbon De Luxe," countered Knievel. "I figured maybe Tommy'd give you something better to do nights than hit the bottle."

Angrily, Will rushed to the sink and dumped out the beer, slamming the glass down on the counter and leaning against it for support. He wanted to shout and scream at Knievel, but he knew he was wrong, and he suppressed his misspent anger.

Knievel reached for his goggles and helmet. "I guess asking you to stay away from the bottle is too much. You're stuck with it. Just like Tommy's stuck with you. Only thing you can do now is treat him like a son."

Will whirled, took a single threatening step toward Knievel. "You're still buttin' into my business. I asked you to keep out of it."

Knievel paused at the door, his hand frozen on the knob. "Pardon me while I butt out." He opened the door and for a moment just stood there, the cacophony of the crowd drowning out his thoughts.

Knievel had to speak loudly to be heard: "You know something, Will. That boy may only be ten years old, but right now he's more man than you are!"

The door slammed shut behind Knievel, and Will Atkins was left with his irreconcilable thoughts. He knew he was wrong but he cursed Evel Knievel. Yet no matter how hard he tried, he could not muster up a feeling of hatred against Knievel. Some forms of love ran too deep.

Gifford again, ladies and gentlemen, to remind you those lions and tigers aren't household pets. Each of those huge cats weighs several hundred pounds. They don't like strangers, especially strangers on noisy motorcycles. There'll be nothing between them and Evel except air, clouds, sun and sky. And as Evel will tell you, he can jump but he can't fly. So we're all in for the most dangerous day of Evel's life.

It was pre-jump interview time, that traditional moment when Evel Knievel permitted reporters and photographers to swarm around him and ask their questions.

"How you feeling this morning, Evel?"

"Like I'm walking on air."

"Don't those four-legged creatures bother you?"

"Not half as much as two-legged creatures."

"How far are you going to jump today, Evel?"

"Just far enough."

"What worries you the most?"

"Taxes and death. In that order."

The photographers and TV cameramen closed in for their exclusive shots. Knievel posed in front of his equipment van, aware that Kate Morgan wasn't among them. Then he saw her, poised atop the hood of her Cadillac convertible, snapping her own special angles of Knievel.

She was dressed more casually than when Knievel had seen her before, but the curves of her figure were as greatly enhanced by pink cotton pants with ankle-bands and flared legs, a yellow pullover T-shirt with multicolor embroidering and an unzippered tan leather jacket with rayon satin lining.

Knievel had trouble keeping his eyes off her and fumbled an answer to one of the questions. He felt hopelessly distracted by the svelte figure, so he told the photographers and newsmen it was time for him to begin preparations for the jump. "That's all for now, men. Thanks for wandering by. Dig you after the jump."

They wished him luck and immediately left for the stadium to pick the best vantage points for their cameras.

Knievel lingered behind, his attention fully on Kate as she climbed down from the convertible. She wiped a speck of dirt from her leg and threw her head back. It was an absolutely gorgeous sight.

Knievel gestured. "You here . . . the other photographers there . . . how come you're always alone?"

"Well, I don't run with packs. Never did, never will." She snapped a quick picture of Knievel, catching him with his mouth open.

"That's one way to avoid wolves," said Knievel with a wry smile.

"And other predators. Like you said, it's the two-legged creatures you have to watch out for."

"Vultures don't go in packs either."

"Or eagles," said Kate.

"You are a girl who can stand on her own two feet."

"And I intend to *stay* that way."

"If you really believe I'm not going to survive today's jump, you have nothing to worry about. Tonight or any other night."

"Stand still," she ordered, taking another picture. She smiled. "I bet that's the first time anyone ever got a picture of you looking petulant."

"You know," said Knievel, watching Kate as she continued to circle him, snapping him from different angles, "I think the only thing different about you is your reason for being here."

"We've both got jobs to do. Right?"

"So you think today's the day I'm going to buy it."

"You said that, I didn't."

"You're really an optimist, you know that?"

Kate strolled past him nonchalantly, throwing one last glance over her shoulder as she hung the Nikon around her neck. He was still watching her, admiring every movement of her body, every toss of her head, when Tommy approached.

"Evel," said the boy, "I think it's time."

"Pretty good crowd, Tommy?" he asked.

"The stadium's jammed," replied Tommy. "Really jammed."

"I'm riding over to see Frank Gifford. See you in a little while." Knievel climbed onto his warm-up Harley and rode out onto the field. The cheer that greeted him was deafening.

You know, ladies and gentlemen, ever since the beginning of time, man has wanted to fly. Well, today we'll be watching the only man alive who does fly ... without wings. I'm proud to call him my friend, and it's an honor to introduce him to you ... the greatest and bravest showman in the world ... EVEL KNIEVEL!

Hiya, Frank. You're looking as great as I've ever seen you. How're you, Evel?

Good as new. Feeling super and ready to fly. Give me that mike for a moment, Frank ... Thanks ... Well, it's nice seeing my old friend Frank Gifford, and it's great to be here with you people in Long Beach today. Before I do the jump, though, I wanna take a minute to talk to you about something that's been bothering me a lot. I see a lot of young people in the stands today and I think it's something that should be said. . . . You know, I go to Indianapolis every year to see the Indy five hundred. I go there with friends who drive and race. Every year when they go there to qualify they usually have to go as fast as they can to get a front-row position. They put nitro in their cars sometimes instead of fuel that's intended to be in the cars so the cars'll go faster. And they do go faster. For five or ten laps. Then they blow all to hell. . . . And you people, you kids, if you put nitro in your bodies, in the form of narcotics, so that you can do better—or so you think you can do better—you will. For about five or ten years.

And then you'll blow. All to hell. So you'd better think twice before you make the decision of what you want to gas up with. . . . You're a wonderful crowd. I'm glad you could all make it today. And I'm going to do my best to make it . . . right across this jump. . . . Frank, it's all yours.

Thank you, Evel Knievel. Ladies and gentlemen, Evel is always risking his life when he jumps, but today he's deliberately raising the odds against himself. Those lions and tigers are untamed killers. Evel must clear that open cage . . . as he tries for a new world's record of one hundred and ninety feet. . . . And now there he is, ladies and gentlemen, the famous Evel Knievel, going through his warm-up paces . . . look at those lions and tigers nervously pacing their cages. They don't like the sound of that motorcycle . . . and they're hungry, eager to sink those jaws into whatever they can find. There he goes, into the pits to change bikes . . . let's give him a great big hand. . . .

"These handlebars don't feel right." Knievel was already astride the Harley-Davidson on which he would perform the jump. Will reached for a wrench, but Tommy already had the tool in his hand and gave it to Will. "Here, Dad."

Will took it begrudgingly, barely glancing at his son. Knievel could sense the helplessness the boy obviously felt in his futile attempts to get closer to his father, so he tousled Tommy's hair. "Tommy, you've got yourself a summer job until you go back to school."

"You mean that, Evel?"

"Like I said. Everyone earns his keep around here."

Ben Andrews felt like burping.

The chili and beans weren't setting well at all. That's what he deserved for rushing through the morning without breakfast and then settling for a quick snack near the main entrance only a half hour before the show was to begin.

Knievel had often castigated Ben for his improper diet. Well-balanced meals were a day-to-day necessity Knievel had stressed from coast to coast, and a lot of people had listened and improved their eating habits as a result.

But not Ben Andrews. Always in too big a hurry, always moving at breakneck speed to consummate one more big promotional deal for Evel Knievel. So Ben Andrews had ended up living on hot dogs, hamburgers, French fries, burritos, and a hundred other greasy junk foods. In turn, he sought "fast relief" with Tums, Alka-Seltzer and Rolaids.

Right now a bicarbonate of soda would have calmed him down, but there wasn't time for such luxuries—not when there were receipts to be counted.

The desk Ben sat behind in the cashier's office was literally covered with money. He ran his fingers through the stacks of bills, imagining a velvet softness that wasn't really there. Ben loved the dollar so much he dreamed of it at night, mentally fondling it the way a man might fondle a beautiful woman.

Ben saw the money as symbolic of another successful jump. Successful in the sense of its monetary return, even if its success for Knievel was yet to be determined. But then, that was Knievel's lookout, not Ben's. All Ben was responsible for was the booking and the receipts that resulted. As long as he fulfilled his end of their bargain, and filled his own pockets in the process, he felt no self-doubts or remorse.

Ben finally burped, tasting the awful aftermath of the chili, and apologized to Eddie, the cashier who shared the office with him. He could hear the crowd as he counted the money, amazed at Knievel's incredible drawing ability. No matter how long he was exposed to the jumper, Ben was amazed.

Ben felt self-righteously smug as he recalled Jessie Hammond's feeble, mealy-mouthed attempt to sway Knievel into Millard's corner. What a waste of time and effort . . . if not brainpower, since Jessie Hammond had little of that to begin with.

Someone knocked.

At first, Ben didn't even notice. It was the sound of Eddie, moving toward the locked door, that jarred him out of his money-minded thoughts and the automatic process of counting stacks of green paper.

"Who the hell is it, Eddie?"

"Don't know, Mr. Andrews."

"Security," came a voice through the door.

Ben looked relieved. So did Eddie.

"Let 'em in," ordered Ben. "I get nervous with all this money lying around here loose like this."

The two men who barged in dressed in the uniforms of stadium security, their revolvers already out of their holsters, were obviously not stadium security officers.

Ben froze in position, his cigar firmly wedged between his teeth. All he could think of was that Knievel was about to make the most dangerous jump of his career for nothing.

Then Ben thought of his own safety, and for the first time

in his life he felt genuine fear, felt something tingle along his spinal column, felt something turn his blood to ice.

Ben recognized one of the men, and for a moment couldn't place him. It had been recently . . . of course, he was the one he'd seen hanging around the rig the day they arrived, the day Evel had demanded his share for the extra seats. The guy had been carrying a camera. Snapping pictures of the trailers. A newspaperman, a photographer . . . hell, that had been a cover. For this. A heist. And he'd been dumb enough to fall for one of the oldest tricks in the book. Maybe he wasn't the hotshot mastermind he'd given himself credit for being.

The man Ben recognized didn't say a word. He just turned on old Eddie, who was due to get his pension in another six months, and fired his silencer-equipped revolver.

The slug that hit Eddie was fired at point-blank range. A roseblossom bloomed above his heart and he staggered back against the wall, knocking loose a *Playboy* calendar hanging there. Eddie was suspended in an upright position for an instant, his arms level with his shoulders, then he reeled forward, reaching out with both hands to find some form of support and moaning a long, slow "ahhhhh."

When Eddie went down he took the flowerpot on the desk with him, and then there were two roseblossoms on the floor.

Ben stared into the smoking barrel of the revolver, which was pointed directly at his forehead. "What do you want?" he blurted. "You don't have to shoot. I'll give you anything you want."

"Nothing," said the "guard." "There's nothing we can't just take after you're dead."

"Wait!" cried Ben, feeling the perspiration rolling down his reddened face. "Let's talk about this. There's more where this came from." He ran his hand across the top of the money—just so there was no mistake what he was talking about. "A lot more. You can have it all."

The revolver barrel didn't waver; neither did the eyes of the grim-faced man who held it.

So this is how it comes, thought Ben. In a split second, when you're least expecting it. Not from your sworn enemies, not even from a rival promoter. But from a punk holdup man who only cares about the money.

Or so Ben thought until the gunman said, "You should've taken Jessie's offer to sell out when you had the chance."

Then Ben realized. Millard! He was behind this. He was

the one determined to have Knievel's profits one way or the other.

This wasn't a robbery. Hell, today's box-office receipts were chicken feed compared to what Millard would get with Knievel riding for him. Taking the money was just a cover so they could knock him off. Then Millard would have no competition. Clear sailing for six record-breaking jumps in Mexico.

And in that instant, Ben knew for certain he was a dead man.

He was right.

The slug caught Ben above the left eye, passing through the brain and emerging through the back of his skull. The impact threw him against the swivel chair. He crashed against the baseboard, his neck twisted askew as the full weight of his body came down in a tangled heap. His straw hat lay at his side, having come off his head during the fall. Ben had uttered no sound.

Norman Clark was stuffing the money on Ben's desk into the canvas bag he had carried into the cashier's office with him.

"Another heist to cover another murder," said his accomplice.

Clark finished stuffing the money into the bag and turned to look at his companion. He found it difficult to conceal his dislike for Nick Barton.

Barton was a tall, muscular man with beady green eyes and a sardonic smile that had been the last thing many individuals residing in or near Chicago had ever seen on earth. His swarthy complexion, topped by unruly, jet black hair, always made Clark feel queasy—like he was looking at someone who hadn't washed in a long while.

Clark had to admit to himself that Barton had done an admirable job bringing in the trailer body from up north, but he still wondered why Millard had brought in outside talent when Clark himself could have driven in the rig. And surely he could have pulled off this little job today without help. Clark was further bothered by the rumor he had heard from Chicago that Barton had once shot and killed a twelve-year-old girl during a robbery. If there was one thing Clark hated, it was someone who would shoot down a child in cold blood.

Clark closed up the sack and set his mouth stubbornly.

"Don't knock it," he told Barton. "It works every time. Now let's get out of here before those shots attract someone."

Together they strolled casually from the cashier's office, a tune from *The Music Man* on Clark's lips.

They passed the two real security guards at their post and gave lazy waves and informal nods of their head.

The guards returned the wave.

"Hang in there," said Clark to the guards and kept on humming.

Let me direct your attention to the far end of the track, ladies and gentlemen. To the east end of the stadium. Here comes the Evel Knievel caravan. Trailers, vans, trucks with Evel's ramps and bikes, and a completely scientific machine shop. And there's the Sky Cycle that almost carried Evel to his death at the Snake River. Almost. That gleaming white pick-up carrying Evel's two favorite jump bikes is custom-built. The only one of its kind in the world. Ladies and gentlemen, you're watching three million dollars of mechanical wonders on parade.

In the vehicle tunnel, Will finished adjusting the handlebars as an impatient Knievel watched. Tommy stood nearby, feeling the anxiety and tension between the two men. Will stepped back. "Okay, Evel, try that on for size."

Knievel climbed onto the jump bike and again felt the comforming of body to machine, and vice versa. He twisted the handlebars and smiled. "That's perfect, Will."

Will shook his head and looked doubtful. "Low, high or sideways, it won't make any difference."

"What's worrying you, Will?"

"Evel, that jump's too long. You'll never make it. You're lion meat right now."

"You heard Gifford . . . I'm going for a new record."

It sounded like a plea, not just a warning: "I'm telling you, Evel, there's a limit and nobody can jump any farther on one of these toys"—Will patted the saddle of the Harley—"than you already have."

Knievel gunned the engine of the Harley. He turned to Tommy, tipping back his helmet. "What do you think, Tommy? We run a democratic outfit here. Everyone speaks his mind. No matter how old they are."

"Well," answered Tommy slowly, "I don't think you should take any dangerous chances."

Knievel put his hand on Tommy's shoulder and gazed at him full in the eye. "Tommy, there're thousands of people out there waiting to see me jump. I said I'd go for a new record and that's what I *have* to do. It's either that or back down. And if I was gonna back down, I shoulda done it before now. Now I owe those people out there too much."

Knievel didn't wait for Tommy to reply; he rode onto the field. The applause was so overwhelming it brought tears to Tommy's eyes.

Will was still watching Knievel, unaware of the emotional effect the day's events were having on his son, when Tommy said, "Dad?"

Will turned slowly, indifferently. "Yeah?"

"Could you teach me to ride sometime?"

Will shook his head emphatically, averting his gaze back onto the field. "Forget it. I'm an *ex*-rider."

It looks like a perfect day, ladies and gentlemen . . . clear skies and a warm sun for all of us, especially for Evel. Weather is as important to him as it is to an astronaut. But the slightest wind change will throw Evel's timing off . . . because a fraction of an inch can mean the difference between life and death when Evel jumps!

. . . Now for the moment you've been waiting for . . . Evel Knievel attempting to jump over an open cage full of jungle killers . . . for a world's record span of one hundred and ninety feet.

The two ramps had been positioned dead center in the field—Evel had insisted on the equipment having a symmetrical look. This was one thing he constantly insisted on, an image of neatness, of show-business glamour, and to his way of thinking, objects off center did not contribute to that effect.

He rode his Harley to the eight-foot masonry wall extending north along the grandstands, following its curve around to the southern end of the field.

He performed a few obligatory wheelies, then sped defiantly past the cage of animals, his rear wheel kicking topsoil that had been brought all the way from Redondo Beach into the cage. The animals roared their anger and showed their annoyance by leaping up on the mesh fencing.

Normally Knievel would have toyed longer with the audience, building up its pitch, but he decided to eschew prolonged preliminaries and get down to business.

There was something extra-sensational about those lions and tigers, something extra-menacing that had put the crowd on the edge of its seats. He already had them in his hip pocket.

Knievel rode to the far end of the field and took the take-off ramp at a fast speed, hoping they would think this was it —that he was starting the record-breaking ride.

But he came to a screeching stop at the top, peering down into the roofless cage. The lions were still growling and pacing anxiously, their tails savagely swishing the air. One of the tigers turned and roared at him, rising on its hind legs, defying him to leave the rampway.

Knievel gazed out over the crowd, realizing for the first time how quiet it had become. Somewhere out there, probably in one of the expensive private booths, Millard was watching—Knievel had seen him and his lawyer, Cortland, arriving in a limousine earlier that day. He thought of Ben Andrews—no doubt in the cashier's office already, counting the afternoon's take. He could read that guy like a book.

And then Knievel saw Kate Morgan.

She was standing near the animal cage, her Nikon loaded and ready. Wonder if she's such a cool lady right now, he asked himself. Wonder just how she feels about her prediction—that this is going to be my last jump; that this was the day I buy it.

Would he make it? Bitching A.

Knievel sized up the distances again. Hell, a guy could do anything if he tried hard enough. He thought it and he believed it but it still failed to dispel all the fear he felt welling up in his stomach, and which threatened to jettison into his throat.

No more time to rationalize it. Just do it. Goddamn it, Knievel, just do it. Get it over with and go drink a beer.

He kicked off and returned to the bottom of the ramp, made a fast wheelie around Kate, winked at her, noticed that her normally rosy complexion had turned slightly pale, and headed for the far end of the stadium again.

Ladies and gentlemen, here comes Evel Knievel roaring down the road to glory . . . making the most spectacular jump of his life.

It was spectacular, and it was graceful, and it was the damnedest jump Gifford and all the others in Long Beach Veterans Memorial Stadium would ever see in all their lives —even Knievel knew that as he rode the bike on its lambent arc.

But it was a bad jump.

He wasn't riding to glory. He was headed for disaster—Valhalla for jumpers who didn't have the brains to know when to quit; who pushed for more than they could deliver.

That's crap! he told himself. You pick your jump and you take your chances. He wouldn't have wanted it any other way.

One thing Knievel was immediately aware of, in addition to the bad position of the bike, was that he had cleared the animal cage. At least he wasn't about to become lion food.

The crowd had turned breathless as it watched this real-life cliffhanger, awed by the jump and unaware of the dangers that were only seconds away.

Gifford knew. He had borne witness to too many of Knievel's hair-raising jumps not to sense that something was wrong with the angle of the bike's descent. "Oh . . ." But the single word that foredoomed disaster was drowned in a sea of spectator excitement.

Seven airborne seconds—that's all it amounted to. Seven seconds in which Knievel was risking all he had worked to build.

The front wheel of the Harley touched the landing ramp. Smoking rubber, an abbreviated squeal, an erratic bike. As at Wembley, Knievel was off center. The bike fishtailed, and he realized the impact had jarred loose the handlebars. Knievel fought to control his landing, but it was strictly a perfunctory action—he knew there was no way to correct the motion at such a fantastic speed.

The Harley literally slid out from under Knievel. He fell onto the ramp in a sitting position, his buttocks making first contact. Knievel continued to scoot along the ramp, like a child riding down a slide.

Fortunately, the bike was out ahead of him and he was in no apparent danger of being mangled by its crushing weight. He felt the friction on his buttocks and prayed that the jump suit would protect him from picking up any splinters. A strange thought for a man in imminent danger of broken legs or a busted neck.

The momentum ruthlessly thrust him forward when he reached the bottom of the rampway. He rolled head over heels with the ease of an Olympics somersaulting champion.

There were piercing, stabbing, tearing sensations. Paroxysms of pain shot through him like high-voltage jolts of electricity. He experienced throes of burning and stinging; his body shook with convulsions as it fought against shock.

The waves of pain were intermingled with a kaleidoscopic combination of colors and images as his body rolled and his eyes opened and closed. He saw flashes of red suns and yellow stars and a universe of speckled dots. The images were brief glimpses of the stadium—a portion of fence, a section of billboard, an area of the grandstand.

Certain pains were too specific for Knievel not to recognize. He realized he had sprained his right wrist—he had done it enough times before. He felt the crash helmet pressed against his face each time it brushed with the ground and he knew he would have bruises to show for each contact. There was a jarring impact to his back and for a second he blacked out.

The Harley sputtered a death gasp. The handlebars had become completely detached and were bouncing across the turf on an erratic, independent course. The front spokes were shattered; the rear axle hopelessly bent out of shape. The foot pegs were twisted beyond recognition.

When Knievel swam up out of the darkness to find himself once again soaked in sunlight, and in some of his own blood, he was no longer rolling. His body, twisted into contortions for which it had never been intended, had come to a complete stop.

So had the stadium. An ungodly silence had fallen over the spectators, who had been so jubilant only moments before.

Kate stood frozen in position by the animals' cage, her Nikon in front of her face, her finger on the button. But she had been too horrified, too transfixed, to take a single picture. "Oh my God," she said over and over. "Oh my God." It was only after Knievel had stopped somersaulting that she had instinctively snapped the shutter. Now she broke into a run, racing for Knievel along with the rest of the photographers and reporters and TV camera teams.

Ladies and gentlemen, please, please, hold your seats. There's plenty of help for Evel down on that field. Please, I urge you to stay in your seats until we can report on Evel's condition.

Tommy wanted to race to Knievel's side, but Will held him back. "This isn't for kids," he shouted, restraining the urge to shake the boy, perhaps even slap him to make him understand.

Tommy continued to struggle. "But he's my friend."

"How do you think I feel—"

The boy broke away from Will's hold. Will could have restrained him, but had decided to let Tommy respond to his emotions. Because that's what Will wanted to do: rush to Evel's side. He immediately ran after Tommy.

In their box seats, Millard and Cortland watched—Millard with a deep concern, Cortland with his standard air of indifference.

"If he dies," rasped Millard, "we're in a helluva fix. I need Knievel in Mexico. Alive!" He turned to Cortland. "Get on the phone. I want the best orthopedists and neurosurgeons in town standing by and available."

Cortland was already moving. "The best," Millard repeated. "Nothing but the best."

Near the wreckage of the Harley, a twisted, mud-spattered mess of metal, lay the equally twisted body of Evel Knievel.

A large crowd had already gathered around him as Kate pushed her way through. Everyone was afraid to touch the daredevil—they had formed a circle around his prostrate body, watching for some sign of life, some movement, anything to tell them their hero was going to survive this jump as he had survived so many jumps before. Among those spectators on the field were a handful who hoped he would never move again. They were the blood seekers, and they were the undesirables that could be found in any stadium crowd.

Kate went right to Evel's side, reaching out in hopes her fingers would find a pulse, no matter how faint.

She was greeted with a wink.

And the beginnings of a smile.

Somehow, though his body was battered and bruised, and wracked with spasms of pain, and perhaps even on the verge of death, Knievel had managed that much.

He managed more. His lips moved. "Sorry, mzzzzz," he said hoarsely, almost inaudibly. "I'm still alive . . . Better buy . . . more film."

Tommy was running ahead of Will, who was out of condition and puffing badly. They reached Knievel at the same

90

time as a doctor and an attendant with a folded stretcher. Gifford, microphone still in hand, was right behind Will and Tommy.

Evel Knievel had closed his eyes again and was resting his head against the ground when he became aware of a roaring. At first he thought it was the crowd. But it was not a human noise. He considered the possibility it was a ringing in his ears. No, this sound was too familiar. This was a sound he knew all too well.

It was the Harley. The damned thing, despite the impact it had absorbed, despite the damage to its gears and other working parts, was still talking to him, telling him it too was alive.

If that goddamn bike can stay alive, Knievel thought, so can I.

Now Knievel heard voices, and he opened his eyes again to see other faces he knew besides Kate's. There was Will, and Tommy. And a new sound.

A siren.

He was familiar with that sound too. The men in the white suits were coming for him again, he mentally chuckled to himself, surprised he was capable of such levity at a time like this. Having experienced so much pain before, and becoming familiar with it, had perhaps made him giddy. He was suddenly aware that the pain had subsided—shock was setting in. But the pain would return. It would creep up on him softly and then scream in his ear, and Knievel would scream back silently, and they would be reunited as one.

He felt a surge of new strength when he saw the face of Frank Gifford above him, holding his microphone, and he thought he could see the birth of tears in the sportscaster's eyes.

Someone else was bending over him. A man in a gray flannel suit. Receding hairline. An omnipotent, supercilious figure. Doctor? Sure as hell couldn't be an undertaker. Not yet anyway.

"Will . . . Will." Weakly.

"I'm here, Evel."

"We've got to get him into the ambulance," a man said.

Knievel tried to place this man, then saw the drawn, tormented but familiar, face of Will. Moving lips. "You gotta go in the ambulance, Evel." It was a sepulchral voice. As deep as a bottomless grave.

"Will, please . . . I wanna talk . . . to the people."

"He's got to be kidding."

"Shut up." Had Will or Gifford said that? The voices were fuzzy.

The man who might be a doctor was adamant. "He can't do it . . . he'll just tear himself up worse."

Will's arm came across the man's chest, moving him back out of the way, authoritatively but gently. Then the arm was coming down to touch Knievel, to pick him up gingerly, carefully, like hands preparing to dissect a million-dollar diamond, or hands preparing to carry out a delicate heart operation. Those benign, skilled hands brought him to his feet. He was being turned slightly, so that he was facing Frank Gifford.

"Over here, Frank." Will's voice. Knievel was sure of that now.

Something was being extended to him. He took it. Cold metal, but warm. "Thanks, Frank," he said, not seeing the sportscaster clearly, but knowing he had to be there because of the warmth of the microphone.

There was fuzz on his lips and he had to spit it away before he could speak: "The accident . . . the fall . . . doesn't hurt so much. But . . ." Knievel closed his eyes, for the ground was swaying, moving, buckling.

He steadied himself with Will's help. ". . . But after all these years, trying to get up and walk away from it . . . that's what hurts . . ." He wasn't sure if he had said that correctly. He suddenly felt tired, exhausted, like a young boy who has been lost on a snow-covered mountaintop for a week and who yearns to see home again. He wanted to lie down and go to sleep. Forget about crowds. About bikes. About jumping. "You've . . . you've probably seen my last jump."

He heard the murmur of surprise, the outburst of disappointment. The microphone fell from his hand as the crowd recovered and burst into a thunderous ovation.

"Okay, now get the stretcher." Will again, to the man who might be a doctor.

Knievel wanted to shake his head, but he was afraid the ground would open up and swallow him. "No," he insisted, "I came in walking . . . help me walk out."

Using only Will as support, Knievel began walking toward one of the exits. Each step seemed like a heartrending achievement to the fans.

"Gentle, gentle," urged Will. "Take it slow and easy."

Gifford picked up the fallen microphone. He stared at it for a moment, overcome by Knievel's pronouncement. It was the last thing he had ever expected of Knievel.

Evel's on his feet, ladies and gentlemen. He's standing! He's walking out of the stadium. We don't know how seriously he's hurt. He told us he walked into the stadium and he wanted to walk out under his own power. He took a tremendous crash. He was traveling at over ... perhaps ninety miles per hour. We'll try to get a report on his injuries later on. Well, he's done it again. Once again Evel Knievel has risen from the ashes of disaster. Once again he has overcome tragedy!

In his loge seat, Millard formed his fingers into the shape of a tent and rested them lightly against his pursed lips. Anger welled within him, but he refused to show it as Barton entered the box.

The gunsel from Chicago was now dressed in gray corduroy slacks and a sport short unbuttoned to reveal an expanse of thick black hair covering his chest. He took the seat next to Millard.

"Everything went exactly as planned," he told Millard. "Ben Andrews won't be giving you any more trouble."

"A lot of good that's going to do me now," countered Millard, keeping his voice as calm as possible. "Knievel's decided to give up jumping."

"So we use a little *friendly* persuasion."

"You don't persuade a man like Knievel. He's got to make up his own mind."

"Where does that leave us?" asked Barton.

"I don't know," said Millard. "But somehow we've got to get Knievel down to Mexico. Right now the best thing we've got going for us is Jessie Hammond."

12

Convalescence

THE idea that he was drifting, with no solid support beneath him, was his first conscious thought.

He smelled the antiseptic as the fingers of his mind reached out to clutch some firm substance—there flashed before him the images of bleached, grim faces behind white masks; of fluorescent light gleaming off scalpels that worked deftly up and down, back and forth; of pumping machines that produced strange regurgitation sounds; of muted, imperious voices lost far away in a vacuum.

Other recollections: the clinking of tubes and bottles; the glint of needles, the effluvium of light and sound around him.

It all came back to him in a single thought, and he knew it was only his mind that drifted, not his body, and he disentangled himself from fear and settled into something soft and pillowy and he knew he wasn't anywhere in the world but in a hospital bed.

He groaned and emerged from the twilight in which he had been drifting. His peace of mind was shattered when he remembered the pain. It had been an unwelcome night visitor. Its arrival had been followed by the scurrying of bodies around his bed, the sensation of a cool liquid on his buttocks, of a slight jab and a soothing promise that the pain would abate. Some of it did leave him, but enough lingered to make him want to cry out. He had refused—he had gritted his teeth and kept it an internal affair. It was the price one paid in the jumping business to maintain a professional stance.

He must have groaned as he shifted slightly, for he heard a familiar sound—at least there was some vague recognition of his own voice.

Evel Knievel opened one eye.

What he saw was not pleasing to a man who hates hospital rooms. The eggshell-white walls surrounding him formed a framework of sterility that threatened to engulf him. He hated sterility and the lack of all primary colors but felt less intimidated when he turned his head slightly and saw a dozen red roses and a dozen yellow roses at the foot of his bed. He also saw stacks of telegrams piled on a white tabletop by the hundreds. Well-wishers from all over the world had read about the Long Beach accident.

He realized he was not a pleasant sight. He dropped his eyes to his chest to find it encased in a cast. His right arm was resting in a sling and he felt the wrappings on his broken collarbone. He ached from head to foot, and knew he was covered with bruises. Well, he thought, remaining the eternal optimist, it might have been worse. He might never have awakened at all.

He saw Will and Tommy Atkins standing at the door to his room and bade them enter with a slight nod of his head and as big a smile as he could muster. "Don't hang back," he said, "it isn't catching."

"Yeah, Evel," said Will.

"Hi," said Tommy.

"Hi, yourself. Sure feels good to wake up in a hospital."

"Yeah, I know," said Will, finishing for Knievel. " 'At least I know I'm alive.' " It was something Knievel said every time he awakened after an accident.

Knievel wanted to tousle Tommy's hair, but was afraid the movement would send a new wave of pain down through his body. "Sorry, Tommy. This is turning out to be a pretty nothing vacation for you." They exchanged the barest of smiles.

Tommy came a step closer. If ever Knievel had seen a heart hanging on a sleeve, this was it. That was the thing about youthful innocence—there was no guile to confuse the issue.

Tommy said, "I'd rather be here with you and Dad than anyplace else in the world."

Knievel gritted his teeth again, trying to find a more comfortable position without having to move all the delicate parts of his battered body. "That's about . . . the biggest . . . compliment been paid me in a month of jumps."

Knievel stared at Will, who remained a few feet behind Tommy, hesitant and unresponsive. He wanted to shout at Will, urge him to go to Tommy.

But if Will could read his expression, he wasn't showing it. He stayed where he was, silent and unmoving.

Evel performing a practice jump on his custom designed and engineered stunt ramps.

This composite photo gives a rare view of the many stages of a successful leap.

Evel explains the details of Will's essential equipment check to Tommy.

Evel doing the warm-up wheelies that are his trademark.

Evel gives the high sign to the crowd before takeoff.

Evel attempts a world distance record—over an open cage of hungry man-eaters.

Having cleared the danger zone, Evel comes in for a precarious landing.

Evel astonishes the crowd by walking away from another bone-crushing accident.

Evel, in disguise, convinces Will to wait until the time is ripe for action.

The time is ripe! Evel frees Will from the clinic on the powerful new stratocycle.

Evel makes the most daring jump of all—landing on top of a moving truck.

And uncaring? Knievel wondered.

It was only with the greatest effort that Knievel raised his right hand and extended it to Tommy. The boy took Knievel's hand in both of his, holding tight. Knievel winced but only internally, thinking the pressure was going to drive him straight up one of those antiseptic walls. But he wasn't going to let Tommy know that . . .

"How bad am I, Will?"

"Not so good . . . not so bad." Will shrugged. Same answer to the same question every time. Even the shrug was the same. They'd have to get together a vaudeville routine someday.

"That's good," said Knievel.

"Ben's not so good," said Will hesitantly.

"Ben? What's wrong? He forget how to count?"

"Evel, Ben's dead."

"Dead?" Knievel's voice went numb. Suddenly the minor pains in his body were gone, forgotten, as a new kind of pain took over. One that would take far longer to dispel than any physical ailments. Ben Andrews had been no saint, but he and Knievel had become close during the past ten years, during which time Ben had distinguished himself as the best, and the most flamboyant, and sometimes the most volatile, of jump promoters.

For a long time no one spoke. Knievel digested the news, cleared his throat and turned back to look at Will. "What happened, Will?"

"A couple of guys dressed as security guards busted into the cashier's office just before the jump. Killed Ben and the cashier, Eddie. Got away with most of the receipts from yesterday's gate."

"Do the cops know who did it?"

"Just two guys. Nobody seems to know anything. No clues, nothing. They walked in, killed Ben and Eddie, took the money and walked out again. Just like that."

There was another long silence as Knievel pondered the bad news. He realized that Tommy was staring at him and he elicited a smile by tightening his grip on the boy's hand. "Hey, don't worry. We're all gonna be all right."

His voice permeated with shyness, Tommy said, "Can I ask you something personal, Evel?"

"Far's I'm concerned, there're no secrets in this room."

"Have . . . have you changed your mind about never jumping again?"

97

"Tommy, every person sooner or later has to come to grips with himself. Sometimes it's good for a person to know when to stop."

"But you're not just another person. You're Evel Knievel." The way Tommy pronounced the name, he made it sound like not just a name, but an institution, a tradition, a way of life. Something for thousands of other young boys to look up to.

In his innocence and naïveté, Tommy Atkins had touched the rawest nerve of all.

Knievel's recovery, as usual, was remarkably rapid. By the afternoon that Jessie Hammond came to see him, the doctor had removed the chest cast and had suggested that Knievel take some sun on the hospital grounds.

So Jessie put him none too gently into a wheelchair and pushed him out to a patio designed with many trails for ambulatory patients. They followed one of these trails as Knievel soaked up the afternoon sun.

Jessie childishly insisted that Knievel needed some speed in his drab hospital life and began pushing him at a break-neck pace. "Come on, Evel," he yelled, "you've got more horsepower than that." By then Jessie was popping wheelies with the wheelchair and he and Knievel lost themselves in laughter.

Some patients in pajamas and robes were amused, some frightened, others annoyed at the juvenile display.

One old man was coming up the path, oblivious to their antics, muttering to himself about his recently removed gall bladder. Jessie saw the old man almost too late, snapping the wheels hard to avoid a collision. The wheelchair spilled its contents onto the lawn, sending the old man into a fit of laughter, his gall bladder forgotten.

It wasn't so funny to Knievel, but he laughed after he got over wincing. "You okay, Evel?" Jessie helped him back into the wheelchair.

Knievel managed a smile. "Yeah, I just hit my funny bone. I never thought I could pop wheelies in one of these."

"I better take you back upstairs before they declare you a menace."

Knievel stretched out on his bed, pulling the covers up over his chest. "Boy, it sure felt good getting back out into that sunshine, Jessie. Even if you are a lousy back-seat driver."

Jessie stood at the foot of the bed, pointing to a pitcher resting on a tray. "Listen, how about some orange juice?"

"Yeah, I'll take a glass."

As Jessie filled the glass, he asked, "Evel, have you thought any more about quitting?"

The question touched the raw nerve again. Knievel accepted the glass of orange juice from Jessie, but didn't immediately drink. He opened his mouth to speak, but Will answered for him from the doorway. "Talk about quitting? That's *all* he ever does think about."

Knievel waved Will into the room. "For a fact," he said, sipping the orange juice. It had a bitter taste. Everything about this hospital tasted bitter.

"I'll have to tell you guys something. I don't know what's the matter with me. I shoulda never said I was gonna quit. I didn't really mean it. You know, every time I fall off that horse, what I feel in my legs and my back and my arms is telling my head what to say."

"Maybe you oughta listen," suggested Will.

Knievel gave the empty glass back to Jessie. Jessie refused to give up: "Evel, have you quit liking money?"

"That'll be the day," snorted Will.

"Now you're kidding," said Knievel, pulling up the covers tighter.

Jessie said intensely, "Making that Mexican tour is like being handed the keys to Fort Knox. Evel, all you have to do is take the money and run. Think about that."

Knievel was only half joking when he said, "Oh, I *will*."

Jessie turned toward the door. "Let me know, Evel. But it's gotta be soon." His final glance at Knievel suggested that the daredevil would be an utter fool not to accept Millard's offer. Then he was gone.

Will walked to the bed, pouring Knievel another glass of orange juice.

"What do you think, Will?"

Will put the pitcher down. "Listen, lots of guys are jumpers, and they do all right . . . till they're hurt. Then they quit. But not you. You crash. You burn. You crash and burn again. Over and over. That's what makes you Evel Knievel. I don't think you're ever going to change."

"Are you trying to tell me I shouldn't quit?"

99

"Oh no. I'm never gonna tell you anything like that. It's your life that's on the line but I want you to know, whatever you do decide, I'm with you."

There was dead silence for a moment, as though neither had another word to say. And then it came: Knievel's smile brightened the room and swept back the sterile walls and overpowered the smell of antiseptic.

"Viva tequila!" he shouted at the top of his lungs, frightening a nurse in the next room so severely she spilled her tray favors all over a hernia patient.

"Viva Knievel!" shouted Will with equal verve.

A few minutes later, while Knievel and Will were discussing preliminary arrangements for the Mexican tour, Kate popped into the hospital room.

She looked naked to Knievel without her camera, and he also noticed that the arrogance and combativeness of their earlier meetings was now absent.

She was dressed in a purple floral-print jacket dress and looked more feminine than he had ever seen her look before. He liked it and he thanked her for contributing so much color to the barren room.

"I just wanted to say hello," said Kate, in a voice that was warmly genuine and sexy. Things, decided Knievel, were looking up all over.

"How are you?" asked Kate.

"I keep healin' . . ."

"That's good news."

"Thanks, Mzz. Sit down and take a load off."

Kate took a chair beside Knievel's bed. "I won't stay long. I have another reason for being here."

"What's that?"

"We started out all wrong and I don't want to end it that way."

Knievel smiled the smile of a child. "So . . . don't let it end."

Kate became more businesslike, injecting a certain wistful note into her voice. "Have to. I'm heading out to cover a revolution in South America."

"What's special about that? There's always a revolution in South America."

"And I always come up with some great pictures."

"Hang around," suggested Knievel. "I'll turn more revolutions than anything you'll find in South America. I'll make more noise than you've ever heard anywhere before."

Kate was caught off guard; she hadn't expected to hear such braggadocio, not after what she had seen in Long Beach. "But I heard you say it. That you'd never jump again."

Knievel was grinning boyishly again. "Just changed my mind. We're on our way. To old May-hee-koh." He gestured at Will. "Phone Frank Gifford, Will. Tell him it's fiesta time. Give him all the details about the first jump."

As usual, Will wasted no time in responding. "Consider it done."

After he was gone, Knievel felt some of the old fun flowing back into his tired body. "You like Mexican food, don't you?" he asked Kate.

She threw her head back. "I can take it or leave it."

"I want you to send a telegram."

"Who to?"

"Your editor. Tell him you have a previous engagement—covering bike jumping in Mexico."

The Errol Flynn bar had a slight chip in one of its corners, but Stanley Millard's guests were too enraptured by the Hollywood elegant setting to notice. They had also been plied with enough alcoholic beverages and hors d'oeuvres to put them in a highly positive, and receptive, state of mind to the proceedings.

Millard was concentrating on the piece of paper in front of him. He pretended to read it one final time, but he was really listening to the snapping cameras, the inane conversations and the voices of Cortland and Hammond, which came from behind him. He felt the presence of Evel Knievel near his left shoulder and experienced a slight uneasiness.

The photographers bore down on Millard as he flipped back the last page and poised the pen above the paper.

No, not a paper. A contract. Not even a contract. A means to an end. The fulfillment of a dream.

Millard felt Knievel brush his left shoulder as he too peered curiously down at the final page, at the blank space for signatures. Six jumps for one hundred thousand each. Over half a mil. That's how it looked to Knievel. But what the jumper didn't know was that he was signing his own death certificate.

Cause of death: Too dumb to know what the hell he was getting into.

Millard became aware that one of the reporters was speaking to him and he looked up as pleasantly as he could, inwardly annoyed at these dumb people and their dumb questions and their dumb curiosity.

Stick around, he thought, I'll give you something really good to run in your papers in a few days.

". . . true that Mr. Knievel is getting a record fee for these jumps, Mr. Millard?"

As if to reply, Millard scrawled his signature on the contract. "Yes, and I believe I'm lucky to have him at any price." He extended the ballpoint to Knievel, who removed his right arm from its sling and accepted it.

Millard wanted to wince at the next question, but maintained his smile.

"Evel, do you really feel well enough to jump again?"

Knievel's answer was terse but friendly. "Come on down to Mexico and find out."

Always keep the yokels happy, thought Millard. No need to offend a paying customer.

With the question-and-answer session over, Knievel wasted no time in signing his name. He dropped the pen on the top of the contract and returned his right arm to its sling. He straightened up just in time for the final question.

"Evel, haven't you ever thought of retiring?"

"Yeah," he said, "every time I crash."

Oh, you'll crash all right, thought Millard. Only this time you aren't walking away from it. No way . . .

13

Interview

THEY'RE *saying that whole thing at Long Beach, about you announcing you'd never jump again, was a publicity stunt, concocted by your people to build up a lot of hype for future jumps.*

What'd you say your name was?

Davis, Ken Davis, San Diego Star.

Well, Davis, old buddy, let me tell you something. At Long Beach, I was in a state of shock when I announced I was quitting. It was my body talking, trying to protect me from myself. Naturally, as soon as I came out of the shock, I realized I just couldn't retire. So the answer is no, there was no publicity hype connected to any of it.

I'd like to clarify all this by adding that I'm usually not in the business of saying something unless I mean it. Wouldn't last very long if I did, not even with you journal jocks. Once you tell folks you're gonna do something, you damn well better try or take up needlepoint or some other safe occupation, because the crowd'll tear you apart if you don't.

But I hope your readers will understand what my body has been through these last ten years. Sometimes it gets a little weary and says the wrong things to me.

There's speculation in the sporting world that your late promoter and partner, Ben Andrews, might have been killed by a rival jumper who wanted to crowd you for the number one spot.

I would hate to think so, Davis. I'd hate to see the sport of jumping tarnished. Jumping has become a very popular, and lucrative, sport these last few years. A lot of new young people have tried to claim my number one position, but so far no one's come even close. Killing Ben Andrews wouldn't help a bit. I can't tell you adequately how sorry I was over

103

Ben's death. We spent a lot of years together. So far the police haven't come up with anything you haven't already read in the papers. It was robbery and murder, clean and simple, so it would seem.

They say Frank Gifford is the only announcer you allow in the arenas where you jump.

Not allow. Want. He's the voice that I want to officially represent me. First off, he's an athlete himself. Knows what it's like to get down there in the ring and fight for your life. Originally he was a single-wing tailback with USC, then a defensive back, option passer halfback and flanker-back for the New York Giants. He's now a member of the Hall of Fame. They don't come much better than that. But there's another reason I like old Frank around.

What's that?

Frank is omnipresent. At one time people couldn't turn their TV sets on without seeing Frank squirting foo foo water under the armpits or slapping some conditioner on his scalp. Or showing off his rugged features in the pages of the best magazines. Then he got out there on sports programs. "Monday Night Football" on ABC, stuff like that, and he learned how to call them. So he's got two things going for him. Notoriety and knowledge. I like a man like that. I also rank him as one of my closest personal friends. And I know he throws out good vibrations whenever I jump. Wouldn't do to have a man talking to that many people who didn't throw out good vibes.

This is your first trip down to Mexico to jump, correct?

You hit it right, Davis. I figure the taco concessions should just about cover my expenses.

What do you think of Mexico?

Mexico creates some of the world's most highly prized handicraft and art. She's the world's largest producer of silver and a major supplier of opal, onyx and jade.

What about the people?

Unless there's something about the human race I haven't learned yet, I'd say they're like people anywhere. They like to be thrilled. They like to see a man risk his life. They like to experience vicariously the soaring of bike and man. I know that a lot of people down in Mexico work extra hard for their pesos, maybe harder than folks up north. And maybe that peso doesn't buy so much. So I intend to try hard to make my next six jumps for Stanley Millard six of the most spectacular jumps of all time. That's the least I can do for all the *mamacitas, papacitas, muchachos* and *muchachas* who turn out to see me fly.

Any advice to the young up-and-coming jumpers, Evel?

Damn right. Be careful on those bikes, kids. They can be dangerous if you don't know exactly what you're doing.

I guess the big question everyone always asks is, why do you jump, Evel?

If you were being chased by a ring-tailed tiger and three cougars and came to the edge of a hundred-foot cliff and had no way to go but down, and you knew those tigers were going to eat you alive, what would you do?

I'd jump.

Damn right you would.

14

Viva Mexico

YANKEEISM had reached Mexico ahead of Evel Knievel.

Already the taco business was being jeopardized by the hamburger and hot dog booms, and in every villa and one-horse stop on Highway 45 leading from Juarez to Chihuahua there were drive-in restaurants, root beer stands, low-calorie Pepsi-Cola signs and souped up hotrods traveling north.

Even an occasional *motocicleta* with some black-jacketed *hombre* astride the machine, doing an imitation of Marlon Brando.

"Yankee Go Home" was a slogan of the past—now it was "Yankee Come On" and that meant bring your money and your customs—in that order.

The welcome mat was out not only for *gringos* but for the blond paleface, the *guero* they called Evel Knievel.

Especially the *guero* who defied death, for Mexico was a land of *machismo*, which the North Americans had shortened to "macho." *Machismo*, that childish, nearly psychotic sense of pride that permeated the land, meant speeding faster than the other driver, matching tequila swallow for tequila swallow in a smoky cantina, accepting a cigarette from a stranger even if you didn't smoke (unless you wanted to end up in a drunken brawl) and if worse came to worst, accepting death before dishonor.

It was a land of strange anomalies, for next to each sign of progress (if Pepsi-Cola could be called progress) there were the signs of old, unchanged Mexico: adobe churches, squalid huts, peasants leading burros or donkeys pulling dilapidated wagons, tired old men pushing food carts, women carrying water urns or bundles of laundry atop their heads.

Knievel was aware of the contrast between old and new

as he sat behind the wheel of his Stutz. He was at the head of the motorcade, followed by the trailers, Millard's limousine and the Cadillac pick-up. He was over his injuries, his body felt in tiptop condition, and he was ready to raise hell again.

Northeast of Chihuahua, near the town of Aldama, they pulled into the main entrance of the Rancho Vista Hermosa. It was a massive white adobe structure isolated from the main highway by a high wall and painted the traditional white—like all the other buildings they had passed since leaving the border.

The vehicles came to a stop. At the rear corner of the hacienda, leading to the open end of a patio, were a large group of people who surged forward as soon as Knievel opened the door of the Stutz.

He could tell they were reporters, press photographers (looking no different from their American counterparts), assorted admirers and three officious-looking men he immediately decided were Mexican officials.

As they came closer, with eager smiles on their faces, Knievel realized that the imperious man who led them was Governor Manuel García. The other two were no doubt his aides.

Knievel and Tommy stepped from the Stutz. Millard, Cortland, Norman Clark and Jessie emerged from the limousine and waited behind Knievel. Kate and Will chose to remain in the Caddie until the official greeting was concluded.

The Governor, wearing a freshly pressed vanilla-ice-cream suit, the only touch of color being a red handkerchief peeking from the corner of his breast pocket, extended a hand that was both figuratively and literally warm. Knievel felt his arm being pumped energetically and was thankful he had fully recovered from his sprained wrist.

"*Bienvenida* . . . welcome," shouted Governor Garcia, his jowls and stomach shaking with him.

The Governor was treating him as if they were long-lost friends. Handshakes were important to the Mexicans—they were used for the most casual of meetings as well as the most formal. To behave otherwise would, in the strict *machismo* code, be tantamount to an insult. "Welcome, Señor Knievel. As Governor of this State, I extend our warmest hospitality. We are your servants, *mi amigo*."

Knievel kept pumping the Governor's hand, returning the smile. "Governor, you sound like the good neighbors we're always hearing about up north."

"There are many of us who share those sentiments, Señor Knievel." Garcia gestured to include the officials behind him. "My colleagues, Señores Lopez and Santana of the National Tourist Office, are here to offer their full cooperation. They begin by placing the Rancho Vista Hermosa at your complete disposal."

"Muy bien, amigos," grinned Knievel. *"Gracias."*

"Gobernador, I can only echo the sentiments of Evel Knievel," said Millard, stepping around Knievel and shaking the governor's hand enthusiastically. "You *are* the good neighbors who never disappoint us."

Knievel and Millard shook hands with Lopez and Santana and exchanged greetings, smile meeting smile, compliment equaling compliment.

The Governor motioned toward the patio. "There are refreshments and music, señores."

The entire group began to move around the hacienda toward the rear of the patio. Knievel stopped in midstride, recognizing two figures moving in his direction, as bees attracted to honey.

The older of the two—a big, burly bear of a man—was wearing cowboy boots and a white ten-gallon hat and was of Syrian descent. The other was a younger man decidely Latin —tall, sleek as a cat, handsome.

Knievel pointed them out to Tommy. "That big man, he's J. C. Agajanian, one of the greatest racing promoters in the world. Been turning up at Indianapolis Speedway for the Five Hundred since 1948. Never misses a single year."

"I've read about him," answered Tommy. Agajanian was known to racing car fans of all ages the world over.

". . . And that's Gene Romero with Aggie. He's a great motorcycle racer. He's doing jumps now. They love Gene here in Mexico."

They all shook hands, again like long-lost brothers, and Knievel introduced the two men to Tommy, whose lower jaw hung open in awe.

"What're you doing down here, Aggie?" asked Knievel.

"Mi amigo . . . I'm soaking up local color. And trying to talk Gene into coming north. To your country, *Estados Unidos.* They're now calling Gene *numero uno,* Evel. Even with my bad accent, you must know what that means. Number one."

Knievel nodded and his voice was gracious, even though in his heart he knew who the real *numero uno* was. *"Mucho gusto*. I heard you're the best in Mexico, Gene. *Que la vaya bien*."

There was a touch of mockery in Romero's eyes, if not in his gentle voice: "*Al contrario* . . . I have been told you are also the best, *señor*."

You sonofagun, thought Knievel, I bet you're thinking the same thing I'm thinking.

Agajanian slapped Knievel heartily on the back. "*Como le va?* How about coming north with us, *amigo?* We can make it a twosome. Two daredevils."

"*Dos Atrevidos*," interjected Romero proudly.

"That's it," agreed Agajanian. "Together you can ride the bikes to glory."

"*Que milagro!*" exclaimed Knievel. "It's a great idea. Nobody's ever had two jumpers in the air at the same time before. When it's over, one of us would have to be *numero dos* . . . number two, no?"

Agajanian shot a look at Romero that was the look of the promoter, who saw in the contest not only sportsmanship and rivalry, but riches. "*Magnifico*. It's an excellent idea, Evel. I wish I'd have thought of it myself."

"When I'm finished here in Mexico," replied Knievel. "Right now I've got six jumps ahead of me. Then we'll talk about it."

"My pleasure," said Agajanian, bowing humbly in imitation of Mexican custom. Then he paused, and in a softer voice said solemnly: "I was sorry to hear about Ben Andrews. He was a rival, but a friend."

"*Gracias*," said Knievel, as Agajanian and Romero hurried away. Knievel put his arm around Tommy and led him toward the patio. "Okay so far, *muchacho?*"

"Neat," said Tommy, unable to restrain the thrill he felt at meeting such personages. "Really neat."

In the Cadillac pickup, Kate was snapping pictures of the welcoming committee through the open window, with Will in the seat next to her. "Evel's a great showman, all right," she remarked. "On or off the field, he puts on a great performance."

"The best," said Will.

"He's been like a father to Tommy. Have you looked at your son lately, Will? He's really having a ball. I think all kids must like to play hooky. Even from their parents."

Will's voice was a showcase of torment. "Tommy doesn't

have any parents." He climbed out of the Cadillac and started for the patio. Kate was right behind him, her camera case slapping against her thighs. She caught up with Will, forcing him to face her. "But *you're* his father."

"Only on the birth certificate." Will averted his gaze, afraid to look at Kate.

"Look," said Kate, "We've just come a lot of miles together. We've done a lot of talking. And you know what? You're not fooling anyone about your feelings for Tommy except yourself. And, mister, you ought to stop."

"You should've been a district attorney, lady."

"I'd have won *this* case, buster." This time it was Kate who stormed away, unable to contain herself.

Will watched her strut away, reminded of the fiery temper his wife, Linda, had so often displayed during their domestic spats. They were alike in many ways ... Will felt a new sense of grief come over him as thoughts of Linda flooded back to him, but realized this was hardly the place to turn dolorous. He buttoned his jacket and moved to join the party.

On the patio, the reception for the Knievel entourage was in joyous throes. Waiters carrying drink-laden trays hurried amongst the guests, passing out the libations while bartenders at three different stations mixed drinks punctiliously. Photographers were busy snapping pictures of Knievel, who kept his arm firmly around Tommy and made it a point to introduce the boy individually to the guests.

Governor García continued to mix gregariously with Millard, Cortland and Jessie, then devoted his full attention to Knievel, leading him to the more important guests one by one and indulging in the most elegant of introductions. Knievel admired the Governor's warmth, sincerity and enthusiasm and noted that he was a *mestizo*—half Indian and half Spanish, one of those prominent Mexicans who control the destiny of the country by serving as politician or businessman. These *mestizos* were known to treat everyone with equal respect—from full-blooded Indians to Yankees.

"I have followed all your exploits with great interest," remarked García, "especially the cannon shot in Idaho."

"Well, *gracias,* Governor, but you haven't seen anything yet until you've seen the jumps I'm planning to do here in Mexico."

The Governor was genuinely impressed—and said as much. A mariachi band, dressed in the typical *charro* costumes of Old Mexico, roved through the crowd, playing "Jarabe Tapatío."

Knievel spotted Will talking to Jessie and waved him over. "Here's Will Atkins," he told the photographers. "This is the man who taught me *everything* I know about bike jumping. Without Will, the show doesn't go on. Will, this is the Governor."

"Nice to meet you," said Will.

"My pleasure, Señor Atkins."

A waiter passed next to Will, who reached over the tray and lifted a drink from it. He drank half of it in a single swallow. Governor García watched him, then burst out laughing. "I see you enjoy our Scotch."

Will almost choked on his drink. "I thought all you drank down here was tequila."

"No, señor, I assure you. Only the lower classes, who enjoy not only tequila but *pulque*."

"Never heard of it," said Will.

"*Pulque* is a fermented cactus juice which is widely enjoyed at fiesta time. The middle classes prefer Scotch, which in this country is also eighty-six proof. We also enjoy our rum here, particularly Bacardi. The company was forced to flee Cuba after Castro took over and it has operated here in Mexico ever since."

"What you learn in Mexico," Will said to Knievel.

The mariachi band began a rendition of "Las Golondrinas."

"Come on, boys," Knievel told the photographers. "Get yourself some exclusives." The cameramen pressed in on Knievel, Will and Tommy. The Governor tried to get in his share of viewfinders too.

Will's eyes widened as one of the flashbulbs went off in front of his eyes.

Pop!

A series of bulbs exploded before him.

Brilliant circles of light.

And Will was lying on the floor of the van again. He had forgotten the face of the man hovering above him, snapping picture after picture. But it came back to him now.

Jessie Hammond.

He turned to look across the patio. Standing next to the mariachi band was Jessie, talking exaggeratedly to Clark, Millard's driver, drawing a diagram in mid air. No doubt the progress of one of Jessie's glorious jumps of the past.

112

The flashbulbs continued to pop.

Will saw it all clearly now. Jessie must have put something in the Bourbon De Luxe that night he visited him in the equipment van at Long Beach. He must have passed out and Jessie had returned to take pictures.

Pictures? Of what? That part didn't make any sense. Then he noticed that Jessie was turning to talk to Millard and Cortland. They spoke in confidential whispers, as men who know each other well.

Maybe too well. Maybe more than he or Knievel had realized.

Pop! Will's eyes widened. He weaved, almost staggered; Knievel noticed his strange behavior and steadied him with a strong hand on the shoulder. "You okay, Will?"

"Yeah, I—" Will wasn't sure what was wrong. The ground had tilted slightly, then rectified itself. "Just . . . just felt a little woozy for a moment."

"Take it easy." Knievel turned to the photographers. "I meant what I just said, boys. No Will, no show."

"I'm all right," said Will. "I'm all right." Maybe he was all right, but he knew that something was wrong somewhere.

On the outskirts of Chihuahua, Plaza La Esperanza was an imposing eight-thousand-seat stadium which remained serene year-round except for an occasional Sunday-afternoon bullfight.

It was a graceful arena, an architectural achievement of both sculptural style and function. It sat in a picturesque open field, landscaped with Spanish cedars which swayed in the breeze and stood like sentinels over the green field. The southern end of the stadium was built against a hillside beautifully tiered into a series of gardens blooming with beds of Shasta daisies, German irises, foxgloves, zinnias, bamboo, delphiniums and lilies of the valley. Sprinkled among the flower beds were gigantic *pitahaya* cacti, ocote pines and palm trees.

Knievel spent nearly a half hour drinking in the splendor of the setting, mentally praising Millard for picking such an attractive spot. He began to pace off distances across the playing field, Tommy hurrying to keep up with him.

"You're really like an engineer," said the youth.

"I'm just trying to lower the odds against me," said Knievel, squinting against the sun. The ubiquitous heat was pressing down on him, sapping some of his energy but never his enthusiasm. "I check out everything . . . warm-up . . . the jump distance . . . the landing. Like taking out a life insurance policy."

Knievel kept on pacing; Tommy only kept up with him by taking extra-long strides. "To start with," he explained, "I've got to know how much room I have to pick up speed."

"I never knew you had to do all that."

"You thought I just hopped on the bike and took off? Listen, everything I do today may help to save my life tomorrow."

Tommy nodded with agreement as Knievel said, "A bike's serious business. Maybe you ought to take a ride yourself and find out just how serious."

From atop the launch ramp, which had already been positioned on the field, Will Atkins watched Knievel and Tommy. The pain and anguish of his tormented feelings were evident on his face.

Deliberately he turned away and moved to the edge of the ramp. Making a fist, he struck an upright wooden pillar supporting the launch ramp. It might have been interpreted as a futile blow against the fates. "Okay," he shouted to the workmen, some of whom were Mexican laborers, "these're solid. They'll hold."

As Will began to move away from the edge, he suddenly stopped, fell to his knees and extended both hands, moving them across the wooden surface. "Gimme the sander," he shouted to the nearest laborer. "If Evel's wheels ever got caught in this groove, he'd end up in the bleachers. I want Evel landing on the ramp, *comprende*?"

After the laborer had brought Will the hand sander (not without some sign of fear of this *loco gringo* who demanded such perfection), he went to work on the groove, a thin spray of sawdust spattering his face as he cursed under his breath.

Meanwhile, Knievel was pacing off the distance between the launching and landing ramps. When he finished, he walked to the Cadillac pick-up. In the back were two bikes: A standard Harley-Davidson and a 125 Harley "Baha," a small, slender, graceful machine, less bulky than the one Knievel used in his major jumps.

Tommy was already astride the seat, imitating the roar of

a motorcycle engine, twisting the handlebars like some kind of devilish dirt bike rider.

"Think you can handle it?" asked Knievel, standing near the tailgate.

Tommy caught his breath. He didn't dare hope. Still, he nodded hard several times.

"So you really think you're ready to solo?"

Tommy was too anxious to withhold his answer. "I remember everything you taught me."

"No you don't." It was the harshest voice Tommy had ever heard Evel use, and he saw before him a different man: stern, paternal, severely authoritarian. As Tommy's mouth fell open to this unexpected admonishment, Knievel whipped up his left arm. He was holding a junior-size crash helmet.

"Never ever get on a bike without a helmet." He placed the helmet on Tommy's head, giving it a solid slap so that it slid all the way into place. "Hook up," he commanded. Tommy fastened the chin strap.

Knievel lowered the bike to the ground, waving Tommy onto the field. "Now," he said, "now you're ready."

If Tommy felt any hesitancy, he did not show it. He carefully went through the procedure Knievel had taught him: Test tension of rear-brake pedal. Place other boot on foot peg so heel rests against rubber. Note where toe touches gearshift pedal, for pushing down and for toeing up. Twist throttle a few times to get the feel of it. Make sure front brake lever near throttle can be reached without removing right hand from throttle. Check out clutch lever on left handlebar. Check gearshift for neutral position. Turn on ignition switch. Set carburetor choke. Give kick starter a quick downward motion. Let engine idle. Give it half a minute, like Evel said. Cold engine can miss or stall.

Now you're set.

The Baha lurched clumsily forward, coughing and sputtering.

"Coordinate that throttle," came Knievel's voice from behind him.

Tommy continued to shift through the gears ineptly. Yet the bike stayed erect. And kept moving. "Thatta boy," enthused Knievel. "Just keep it moving."

Tommy Atkins was a proud, fulfilled lad as he rode the spasmodic bike. His confidence built quickly and he began to ride in circles. He couldn't resist the temptation to turn his head to grin at Evel. Maybe even throw him a wave. Show him he didn't have to keep both hands on the handlebars at all times.

Knievel had gone back to pacing the distance between the ramps. He saw Tommy and grinned, raising his hand to join his forefinger and thumb in a circle.

Right on.

Tommy didn't see the oil slick. The Baha drifted into the greasy puddle and began skidding. Tommy froze at the controls, too inexperienced to know how to rectify the bike. He was cool enough to realize that he wasn't about to regain control, so he leaped free just in time to avoid being crushed as the machine capsized.

As he picked himself up, Tommy could see that the Baha was slightly damaged and the motor was still running.

Will bounded down the ramp several yards and then jumped off to fall six feet to the ground. He picked himself up and ran toward Tommy. He was suddenly back in shape, moving with the agility of a track star.

Tommy was just bending over the Baha to turn off the engine when Will grabbed him by the shoulder and whirled him around. He shook the startled boy with both hands. "Look what you've done." He was shouting uncontrollably.

Knievel pulled Tommy away from Will, staring him down, unable to comprehend Will's actions. "You . . . the first time you reach out for your son, you try to shake him out of his shoes."

"Look at this bike," said Will accusingly. "It's a pile of scrap."

"The hell with the bike. Look at your *son*."

"Who told him he could ride?"

"*I* told him he could ride. Look, he skidded. That could happen to anyone." Overcome with emotion, Knievel lashed out with his foot to kick the Baha. "It's a machine," he said, trying to calm himself down. "If it breaks, we replace it. But how're you gonna fix what you're doing to this kid?" Knievel put his arm around Tommy, drawing the boy close.

Will's voice was a warning. "I told you before. *Butt out*."

"If I'd listened to that, Will, you *never* would've seen your son. How do you think he got here? By stork?"

There was a lengthy pause as Will considered. "The school sent him," he said naïvely.

116

"That's what the school *told* him. Because that's what *I* told the school to say."

The waters of confusion parted and, suddenly, it was clear to Will. He stared dumbfoundedly at Knievel, looking like a man who has been duped and betrayed. Because that's exactly how he felt. Any thought of gratitude was as distant as the Arctic Circle.

Knievel continued, jabbing Will's chest with a loaded finger every time he uttered the word "I."

"*I* sent the money for the plane fare. *I* figured ten years was long enough to blame an innocent boy because his mother died when he was born."

"Shut up," said Will threateningly.

Knievel ignored him. "*I* figured if you just saw Tommy once, you'd put your arms around him and it'd be a whole new world for you. But no, not you . . ."

"You've pushed into my life once too often." Will Atkins had never threatened to punch Knievel before, but he could no longer restrain himself. He doubled both fists and brought up his hands in front of his face. Knievel took a step backward and also brought up his fists.

"Any way you want it," said Knievel.

Suddenly Kate was there—like a wedge that dropped from the sky and planted itself squarely between them. Both men had been so absorbed in the preliminaries of a brawl that they had failed to see Kate watching from the grandstand—just as they had failed to see her set down her camera bag and stalk across the field toward them in a bellicose manner. "Stop it," she ordered. "Stop it, you two big apes."

Knievel and Will were so startled to see her that both lowered their arms automatically and looked sheepish—like children caught with their hands in the cookie jar. Kate was boiling with rage, yet she suppressed her anger to speak to Tommy, her voice now controlled: "Tommy, I left my camera equipment over by the grandstand. Will you go over there and wait for me?"

Tommy nodded and hurried off. Kate turned again to face the two men, her hostility still visible even though she now spoke in controlled disaffection: "One more minute and you'd have Tommy running for the nearest orphanage." She turned squarely on Knievel first, her gaze like a bowling ball speeding toward the headpin. "Where do you get off telling anyone how to be a parent? All you've done since *I've* been

117

around is try and convince Tommy *you* should have been his father, not Will."

"What do you know about it," said Knievel sharply. "That's a lie."

Her answer was as sharp as Knievel's. "That's a *fact*. You've been so busy making Tommy's life one big chocolate malt that he hasn't had a chance to get to know his father."

"Yeah," said Will, as though he suddenly agreed with everything Kate had been trying to tell him. He should have kept his mouth shut, for Kate now whirled to face him, rising to a new boiling point.

"Shut up, you . . . you *dropout*. . . . According to you. Tommy doesn't have any parents. How right you are."

"Hey, watch it," warned Will.

"I *have* been watching. I've had a front-row seat at this ugly spectacle and I want to tell you something . . . you're both the worst. Real nothing."

Kate paused only long enough to catch her breath before she stormed away.

She joined Tommy at the grandstand. "Tommy," she said, "I'd take it most kindly if you'd have lunch with me."

Tommy bit his lip, fighting back the tears. Then he managed a nod, even a smile. Kate picked up her equipment bag with one hand and put the other around Tommy.

Knievel and Will watched from the center of the stadium, their fight forgotten, their anger dissipated. Neither looked at, nor spoke to, the other.

Kate had covered the bases all too well.

15

The Duplicate

SIX miles from Plaza la Esperanza, on a narrow dirt road off the main highway through Aldama, was an old abandoned adobe barn. It was occasionally rented out from an aging, tottering *labriego* for Saturday night dances or marriage fiestas. And occasionally the owner rented it to strangers, with no questions asked, when enough pesos were placed in the palm of his outstretched hand.

The old man had asked no questions of Jessie Hammond, and he had turned his head to look at *muchachos* setting off firecrackers in the center of the road when the strange vehicles were driven through the main doors of the barn, and the doors immediately closed.

There, on the verandah of his *masada*, he had turned to his memories of his glorious days with Pancho Villa and soon had dozed off under the midday sun, oblivious to the din from inside the barn. He was fast asleep by the time the black limousine pulled up in front and three men climbed out.

Millard, who never deviated from formal attire, lest it somehow taint his image and reputation, was wearing a gray-striped suit by Angelo of Rome and black shoes by Gucci. He was followed out of the car by Cortland, who looked more indigenous to his surroundings in white cotton pants, a dress shirt without tie and dark glasses. As usual, he carried the briefcase.

The third man was an American who carried an ordinary suitcase and wore the holiday clothes of a Babbitt: white shoes, garish pants, sport shirt, loud blazer.

The work inside the barn came to a stop as Jessie, standing at the door like some sinister sentinel, admitted the three.

They crossed to the trailer, which was an identical match to Knievel's equipment rig. Cortland gestured at the motor-

119

cycles lined up near the wall. "Duplicates of Evel's bikes," he said to Millard.

Near the rear of the trailer were two stepladders paralleling the vehicle. On them stood Barton and Clark.

"This is Andy," said Millard, pointing to the man with the ordinary suitcase. So much for introductions.

"I'm impressed with the setup," said the man named Andy. "Care to explain what the hell it all means?"

"You heard the man, Jessie," said Millard. "Explain."

"Sure, Mr. Millard, sure. Well, the trailer has an inner wall of plywood and an exterior wall of metal."

"That much I can see," said Andy impatiently.

"Just get to the pertinent part, Jessie," ordered Millard. Cortland shifted weight from one foot to the other, as if the briefcase he carried were a heavy burden. In a way, it was.

"Between these two walls is an air space," continued Jessie. "Approximately one and a half inches wide. It's filled with fiberglass insulation which, in effect, wraps the entire trailer in a protective cloak against extremes of heat and cold."

"Now then, this is what's interesting. The metal comprising the exterior wall is made in sections generally four feet in width and length."

Barton and Clark, now at the maximum height of the stepladders, had begun to remove the four-foot sections from the top of the trailer flanking the rear doors.

"Look for yourself," suggested Jessie.

Barton handed one of the sections down to Jessie. Clark began to pull fiberglass insulation from the space between the plywood and metal walls of the trailer. Jessie set the metal panel along the wall as Cortland suggested they try it for size.

Andy put the suitcase down on the rough cement floor and opened it.

Jessie whistled, his eyes widening.

The suitcase was filled with white plastic bags.

Cocaine.

He handed one of the bags to Barton, who dropped it meticulously into the space between the two walls.

"Just like a squirrel stashing away nuts," said Jessie. Millard frowned at Jessie's out-of-place levity. Jessie decided to shut up.

Barton reached into the airspace for the cocaine bag and returned it to Andy, who replaced it in the ordinary-looking suitcase. Andy looked at the rig admiringly, then turned to Millard. "How many bags will she hold?"

"Three thousand," said Millard straightaway. He snapped his fingers, without looking at Cortland.

Like a well-trained automaton, Cortland took out his pocket calculator and punched out some numbers.

"Well," said Millard impatiently, "the figure."

"Fifty million dollars over our investment."

Jessie was stunned. "Fifty million! I don't believe it."

Millard gave him another irritated look. "When you see your share, Jessie, you'll believe it."

"Why this trailer instead of Knievel's?" asked Andy, letting the suitcase hang freely at his side.

Millard pointed to the trailer, almost proudly. "There's no way we could keep Evel's trailer away from him long enough to stash the bags . . . so we built this duplicate. Exactly like Knievel's. Down to the flyspecks in the paint job. I've examined this caper from every angle. This is the only sure way."

Andy seemed satisfied. "Okay. Do you have the money?"

Cortland snapped open the briefcase, flashing its contents with the solemnity of a palace guard showing off the crown jewels. Jessie started to whistle again, realized by Millard's frown that it would be uncourtly, and clammed up.

The briefcase was brimming with money. Thousand-dollar bills. Stacks of them. A fortune, even to a jaded millionaire like Millard. Andy scrutinized the contents, riffled gently through one of the top stacks and nodded his satisfaction. Cortland closed the briefcase and resumed his burdened stance.

"You do have two thousand nine hundred and ninety-nine more bags of this?" Millard asked Andy.

"I'll deliver tomorrow night as agreed."

"The cash'll be ready," promised Millard. "As agreed."

The redhead in the Frederick's of Hollywood leopard-skin bikini looked luscious and wet and she was gripping Jessie's arm almost lasciviously. The girl in the one-piece white crochet knit swimsuit with peekaboo holes strategically arranged clung to Jessie's other arm with equal indelicacy.

The photograph had been snapped just as Jessie grinned, his face all pride, his body all muscle, bulging its promises to the gorgeous bodies of the "admirers."

Will Atkins studied the photograph, shaking his head in the gloom of the hacienda bedroom. Jessie always had considered himself a ladies' man, surrounding himself before each jump with the loveliest girls in the country.

Then, at the end of each jump, if he didn't wind up in the hospital, he had selected the most beautiful and rushed away with her for the weekend.

That's probably where Jessie was right now, this very midnight, shacking up with a señorita, decided Will.

Will had picklocked his way into Jessie's bedroom, convinced there was a conspiracy between Millard and Jessie, and certain that somehow Evel's equipment rig figured in the scheme. But anything beyond that was flight of fancy, the wildest of speculations. Not enough to go to Knievel with and convince him. What Will needed was proof—something that would easily persuade Knievel that dirty work was afoot. But what kind of proof was he looking for? That he didn't know—but he would recognize it if he saw it.

Will rummaged through a chest of drawers, working his way through folded dress shirts, sportswear, socks, underwear. He found nothing. He went to the night table, which contained a single drawer.

Inside he found what he had been looking for.

Photographs.

Scores of them, held together by a rubber band. The top photograph was of him. On the floor of the workshop van, passed out cold, the empty bottle of Bourbon De Luxe beside him. The rest were of the van's interior—from every imaginable angle. Floor, walls, ceiling, work benches, bike positions, spare-parts trays.

"I thought I saw you sneaking in here." A soft voice, not even accusing.

Will didn't have to turn to know it was the voice of Jessie Hammond.

But he was surprised when he did turn, for standing next to the jumper were Cortland and Barton. Barton held a revolver; Cortland seemed to be holding only his breath.

Jessie reached out and took the photographs. "I see you're an admirer of good camera work. But you won't be needing them." Jessie took a step toward Will . . .

16

Knievel's Fury

EVEL Knievel had the look of a wrathful man as he pushed the Stutz with a maniacal fury—which meant he was being twice as reckless as usual.

Like a blowfly gorging itself on bloodred meat, he clung to the maze of dusty, tortuous back roads on the outskirts of Aldama, giving birth to huge clouds of baked dust that clogged the noses, ears and eyes of the Mexicans standing beside the roads as he passed, and that robbed the Stutz of its gleaming whiteness. A few of these peasants cursed him and his mad driving, although deep in their hearts they admired such recklessness. And they would later speak excitedly of the *rapido* white machine unlike any they had ever seen before.

An ox cart and a dilapidated *boyero* were crossing a lane as Knievel hung a blind turn in the throbbing Stutz. He automatically swung the wheel sharply to the left—a reflexive instinct from years of motorcycling. The Stutz fishtailed slightly and slid far around the old man, who stood in the center of the trail dumbfoundedly, unable even to shake his walking stick at the *loco gringo*.

El Instituto de los Malsanos was an enormous Spanish-style clinic set far back in a grove of pine trees amid rolling lush green lawns and extensive shrubbery and flowers. It had the facade of a rich man's hacienda rather than a hospital, which was, Knievel decided, misleading for those unfortunate enough to find their way here.

Knievel swung the Stutz into the driveway, continuing to raise storms of dust as he moved toward the parking area. But he had no intention of parking there—he veered the Stutz and screeched to a stop before the main entrance. He slammed the car door behind him, ignoring the dust that

123

now clogged his own nostrils. He cursed, but for other reasons.

Knievel strode up the steps and toward the main door like a man on his way to face an army of challengers, either all at once or one at a time—however *they* preferred it.

In the main reception area, as antiseptic and as foul-smelling as the hospital rooms he had come to despise, Knievel passed a patient in robe and pajamas being escorted by an enormous male nurse in white pants and white, short-sleeved blouse.

Waiting a few feet beyond was Millard, who stood beside a middle-aged American wearing a long white linen coat and looking officious and doctorly.

Millard extended his hand, looking remorseful. "I'm sorry this happened, Evel."

"I'm Ralph Thompson, Resident Administrator," said the man in the linen coat, extending his hand.

Knievel ignored both hands; there was never time for formalities when he was angry. "This place looks like a training camp for wrestlers," he said derogatorily, indicating the male nurse he had just passed.

"Some of our patients," said Thompson, "require . . . ah . . . firmness."

"Where's Will?"

Thompson gestured toward a door and walked ahead of Knievel. Millard followed.

"He's among friends, I assure you, Mr. Knievel."

"Drop the mister and call me Evel."

"This is an American sanitarium staffed by Americans accepting only American patients."

Knievel walked past Thompson to set a brisker pace. "Boy, you sound too good to be true."

Knievel was trying to keep from exploding in rage and frustration as Millard said, "The police who found him recognized him from the news photos. They contacted *both* you and me, luckily."

There was heavy sarcasm in Knievel's voice: "Oh, yeah, he's awful lucky."

When they reached the nurses' station, a wire enclosure that housed the sanitarium's main telephone switchboard, Thompson spoke to an attendant through the mesh screen. "May I have Mr. Atkins' chart, please?"

The attendant pushed the chart through an opening in

the mesh. Thompson studied it thoroughly, then they continued down the hallway.

"I had him brought here because I knew I could trust Mr. Thompson to be discreet," volunteered Millard.

Knievel stopped in the center of the corridor and whirled to face Thompson, angrily asking, "What're you? A doctor?"

Thompson shook his head. "I'm a therapist and I've had extensive experience."

Knievel was still in agony as he turned and resumed the walk down the corridor. "I'm telling you, you're both wrong. Dead wrong. If there's one man I know like a book, it's Will Atkins."

"I wish you were right, Evel. I felt the way you did. So I had the local police check." Millard withdrew a folded sheet of teletype from his pocket. "Here's proof positive, I'm sorry to say." He handed the paper to Knievel. "It's a copy of Will's arrest record back in the States."

Millard exchanged a fast look with Thompson as Knievel yanked the paper from his grasp. He unfolded it, glanced at it, and for a moment the fury went out of him. He sagged slightly and looked beaten. The weight of the evidence in the teletype was, on the surface, overwhelming.

"This way," said Thompson, pointing to the far end of the hall. They continued in silence, Knievel glancing at the teletype again.

The group stopped in front of a door with thick shatterproof and soundproof glass. Knievel moved directly in front of the glass.

What he saw froze his blood.

Will Atkins had gone mad.

He stood in the center of his soundproof padded chamber, dressed in the nondescript green bedclothes of a patient, walking in ever-widening circles like a man stalking prey.

Then Will opened his mouth and began to scream—it was a soundless, hopeless scream, and it was one of the most frightening things Knievel had ever faced. Mangled bodies in race-car crashes and motorcycle mishaps were one thing, but the wreckage of a diseased mind was something he had never been able to comprehend and accept.

And then Will was rushing at the window and pounding on the unbreakable glass, his mouth still agape in a never-ending scream against humanity. The mouth finally closed,

125

and Will stood at the window, staring at Knievel, seeing him but not recognizing him. His sweat-drenched hands were pressed up against the glass.

"I'm going to switch on the speaker," said Thompson, throwing a small switch built into the wall next to the door of the chamber.

Knievel could hear Will's voice now, incoherent, yet a key to his troubled past that now dominated the present. "Why'd you have to die, sweetheart? I'm nothing without you, Linda, nothing." Will moved in circles again and suddenly came to a standstill in the center of the bleak room, throwing up his hands as if to shield himself from some invisible attacker. "I'm gonna crash," he screamed, "gonna crash!" Will bent forward as though yielding to some overpowering pressure on his back. His knees began to buckle. His body trembled, then straightened up again, the crash he had just relived fading away to become a distant nightmare.

Will's voice was in mourning again. "I ruined it between Tommy and me. Tommy, I always wanted to be with you. First I was mad because your mother died." His voice trailed off into indistinguishable sounds. It was only when he modulated it again that Knievel could hear. "Then I figured it was too late. Maybe you were better off without me."

Will began to move again and, reaching one of the walls, struck it with the palm of his hand, then his fist. "Everything's been wrong since the day my wife died." He struck the wall again and again. "I chased my own son away."

Will stopped pounding, turned to face the glass and said in a voice that revealed complete defeat, "Tommy, I love you, Tommy. Love you love you love you . . ." He sank down out of Knievel's sight onto the floor.

"What the hell is all that?" Knievel asked incredulously, his voice unable to conceal the fact that seeing Will like this was one of the most shattering moments in his life.

Thompson cleared his throat, still wearing the officious look. "He took an overdose of something. We don't know yet what it was. If we're fortunate . . . he may come out of it . . ."

Knievel turned to see that Will was on his feet again, walking in circles. After a while he returned to the glass and stared at Knievel, looking at him as though he were a total stranger.

126

Knievel turned on Thompson, glaring daggers. "There's something rotten here." He thrust an accusing finger against the glass. "If he got in trouble drinking, okay, I'd buy that. But *dope*?" Knievel shook his head. "No way, no way on God's green earth."

"All you have to do," said Thompson complacently, "is look for yourself."

"You look," hissed Knievel. "I know that man. Don't try and tell me he's an *addict*."

Millard yanked the teletype from Knievel's fingers, touching it as though it were some sacred document. "Here're the facts, Evel. In black and white."

"I'll need a helluva lot more facts than those before I believe Will Atkins is a junkie."

Now Knievel's attention was riveted back on Thompson. He placed a threatening finger on the doctor's well-starched linen jacket. "Since you're the head honcho at this . . . *oasis* . . . you listen good, doc. You treat Will right. I don't care what it costs. Give him the best of everything."

"You don't have to worry about a thing," said Thompson reassuringly.

"Like hell," snorted Knievel. He turned to give Will one final glance before he stormed down the hall.

Knievel's experience that afternoon at El Instituto de los Malsanos would take years for him to shake.

And then, on certain nights, he would awaken to remember it, his body bathed in the cold sweat of fear.

17

Tommy's Despair

THE voice coming from the other side of the door was urgent, and it carried within its softness a deep-felt concern. "Tommy? Are you in there, Tommy?"

The boy on the bed stirred only slightly. With the shades tightly drawn, the sparsely furnished bedroom was in deep shadows that only added to the boy's misery.

Tommy said nothing, just continued to stare down into the bedspread embroidered with Mexican bullfighters facing charging *toros*.

The door opened slightly, admitting a shaft of light from the corridor. Tommy saw a figure outlined against the light of the hallway and his grief momentarily lifted away from him.

Kate!

"Tommy, are you here?"

"Yes," replied Tommy listlessly, his excitement dying as instantly as it had been born.

Leaving the door ajar, Kate moved toward the bed.

She found him in his clothing, on his side. He rolled over onto his back and stared at the ceiling. Kate restrained the urge to throw her arms around the boy and hold him tightly to her bosom. "I heard about your father, Tommy. I'm awfully sorry."

Finally Kate reached out, realizing that words would not be enough to bridge the gap of misery that isolated Tommy. She touched him gently and sat on the bed next to him. "I just want to be your friend, Tommy. Please, let me help."

Tommy leaped up, shouting bravely. "He didn't do it, Kate." His voice was fierce—with pride, with outrage. "He didn't do it." His eyes blazed and Kate felt a surge of strength —at last Tommy had stopped moping and was fighting back against the shattering news of his father's illness. His voice was full of passion as he continued: "My dad's not a drug addict." Harder: "He's not a drug addict. I'll show you, Kate, I'll show you."

"Show me," she urged, "go ahead and show me."

Tommy crossed to the chest of drawers and took out his scrapbook. "They said my dad was arrested lots of times." He opened the scrapbook, flipping the pages with a frantic urgency. "That's a lie, Kate. I know everything about my dad. Even if he had been arrested, I would have put it here, in this book. No matter what he would have done. I would have put it here."

He offered the scrapbook to Kate. "Try and find it. Go ahead. You can't find it. Because he was never arrested."

Kate couldn't bear it any longer. The boy's heartbreak had reached her and was crushing her. She knelt and stretched out her arms for Tommy. But Tommy was beyond being pitied. He pushed past her . . . and bumped into Knievel.

Tommy stepped back in surprise. Even Kate sucked in her breath—she hadn't heard him entering the bedroom.

Knievel ruffled Tommy's hair. "You're right, little guy. And I'm with you. All the way."

"So am I," Kate reassured him, taking a step toward Tommy.

"Tommy," said Knievel, with a sincerity that could not be mistaken, "nobody on this sweet earth knows your dad better'n me. . . . I agree with you, Tommy. He's not the addict type. In all the time he's been with me, I would have seen it. Some things you can't hide from your best friends."

Tommy's hopes climbed. To an uncluttered and ingenuous mind, the solution seemed simple, and he took a step toward the doorway. "Then they can't keep him in that place. Let's get him out, Evel."

Knievel hated to do it, but it was his sad task to stop Tommy from walking out the door.

As Tommy reached the door, Knievel took him gently by the arm. He spoke softly, quietly, convincingly. "It isn't that simple, Tommy. It's gonna take a while."

Tommy's hopes were dashed and now his battered emotions were strained to the snapping point. Bewildered, he cried out, "But you said you don't believe them."

"Look, Tommy, try to understand." Knievel knelt down next to Tommy. "They're holding all the cards. They've even got an arrest sheet from back home. It's pretty strong evidence."

Every fiber in Tommy's being protested. "But it's not true, Evel. It's just not true."

"That's what I've got to prove, Tommy. I've called the States to have it checked, but it'll take a day or two. I stopped here first because I was worried about you, tiger." Knievel stood up and looked at Kate as he acknowledged her gallant efforts to help the boy. "But I see I was worried about nothing. You're in the best of hands."

Knievel continued to gaze at Kate, and although they stood five feet apart, they were as close as a man and woman in each other's arms.

Kate stepped softly to Tommy and placed her arms around his shoulders.

"Hang in there, tiger," said Knievel, and he hurried from the room, a man with a purpose.

18

Death's Test Drive

IT was called the Strato-Cycle.

It had the look of a machine of the future, even if its components were contemporary.

It was a prototype jet-propelled motorcycle, certain exterior features conveying the shape of a supersonic aircraft. The exhaust was in the form of a tail with fins, and there was a winglike protuberance from each side of the bike.

A metal housing, roughly in the shape of an American eagle, had been fitted onto the front of the bike and it sloped beneath the handlebars, stopping before it interfered with the driver's seat or the footpegs. This housing was painted with the features and feathers of an angry eagle, its beak open in defiance of anything that stood in its path. In the Knievel tradition, the colors were red, white and blue, with stars speckled irregularly over the surface of the bike.

Under a cloudless sky, Jessie moved awesomely around the machine, examining its features like a boy who has just been given his first bicycle.

"It's the bike of the future," commented Millard. He stood a few feet away with Cortland, carefully gauging Jessie's reaction.

"Out of sight," clamored Jessie. "What a mean machine."

Parked behind Millard and Cortland were the limousine, a trailer van and a Porsche Targa, which Clark stood beside.

"What is it?" asked Jessie. "What do you call it?"

"A Strato-Cycle, Jessie."

"Wicked."

"I had it specially built for you."

Jessie's head snapped around. Pride, vanity and respect—some for himself, some for Millard—were all visible in his single expression.

"You could buy twenty ordinary bikes for what this one cost," continued Millard.

"I believe it," said Jessie.

"Go on. Try it."

"Sure," said Jessie—perhaps too eagerly. Millard smiled, knowing he had succeeded in satisfying and enflaming Jessie's ego beyond his wildest expectations.

Jessie leaped onto the seat of the Strato-Cycle like a man whose life depended on speed. He kicked the jet engine to life. The sound was deafening. Cortland winced and placed his hands over his ears in an exaggerated fashion.

Jessie threw the Strato-Cycle into gear and took off at a terrific speed, a cloud of dust left in his place. As Jessie roared along the desert road, Millard turned to Cortland. "Well, are you still worried about Jessie?"

Cortland shook his head, grinning as the roar of the jet engine intruded on his thoughts. The Strato-Cycle flashed past them—a multicolored streak. The machine turned and came back to where the vehicles were parked, surrounding Millard and Cortland in a fresh cloud of dust. They laughed good-naturedly as Jessie cut the jet engine.

He was like an exuberant child at Christmas. "What a bike. Did you see how it handles? I could clear two hundred feet with this baby, Mr. Millard, no sweat."

"Jessie," said Millard, in a voice that promised him the world, "how would you like to try for the world's record on this bike?"

Jessie liked what he was hearing, but he was also confused. "Evel's doing the jumping . . . isn't that right, Mr. Millard?"

"If Knievel crashes . . . and God knows none of us want anything like that to happen . . . then you'd be there to try for the top spot."

Jessie was silent for a moment as he made personal inferences of Millard's explanation. To say that Jessie was thrilled by the possibilities would have been an understatement. "Okay," said the biker. "If Evel doesn't make it, I won't let you down."

Millard smiled. "I know that, Jessie. No matter how Evel does on this tour, you're my top man from now on." He gestured toward the vehicles. "Now, Jessie, I'd appreciate it if you'd take the Porsche back to town for me. We'll see you later."

"Sure thing, Mr. Millard." Jessie touched the seat of the

Strato-Cycle one more time before he moved toward the Porsche. "Thanks for the ride."

As Jessie climbed into the navy blue Targa, Cortland eyed him closely. "I think Jessie really wants Knievel's number one spot."

"I'm counting on it," said Millard, watching the Porsche pull out onto the dirt road. As soon as the car was gone, Millard signaled the van. The rear doors popped open and Barton was exposed, leaning against a Harley-Davidson.

"I've seen that bike before," remarked Cortland.

"You bet your life you have. That's our ace in the hole." Millard rubbed his hands together with a certain touch of avarice. "An exact duplicate of Evel's jumping bike."

Barton, with Clark's assistance, unloaded the Harley. Barton reached into the van and picked up a radio transmitter, pulling out its antenna.

Clark mounted the Harley, kicked the starter and rode out into the desert at moderate speed.

"He's no Jessie," remarked Cortland.

"This is just a little demonstration I wanted you to see, Gunther. Liven up your day a little."

Barton joined Millard and Cortland, a diabolical smile locked on his face. Clark stopped after a short distance, turned the motorcycle and began his return.

When the Hartley was only a hundred yards away, Barton pressed a stud on the radio transmitter.

Cortland jumped involuntarily as there was a loud, almost grotesque, puncturing sound and a yellow flash of light, which might have been an explosion, radiated for a split second from the front tire of the bike. The tire went completely flat and the bike fell on its side, Clark safely rolling free.

The three of them walked the short distance to the bike, where Clark was already on his feet, staring down at the deflated tire.

"The tire has to go flat at the exact instant that Evel completes his jump," explained Millard. To Cortland, it was suddenly clear.

Barton was still grinning devilishly. "You saw it yourself just now. I can send a signal from a quarter of a mile away ... but I won't be more than one hundred yards from Evel's point of touch-down."

Barton reached out to run his hand along the ruined Goodyear tire. "I'll be dressed as an ambulance attendant.

If he isn't quite dead when I get him into the ambulance, he will be when he comes out. Either way we win."

"I'm satisfied," declared Millard.

"Does Jessie know about this part of it?" asked Cortland.

Millard looked in a bemused fashion at Cortland. He was sharp as a lawyer, but sometimes he had to be drawn a blueprint. "You saw me send Jessie back to town, Gunther. Jessie *can't* know about this. And under no circumstances *must* he find out. He still feels loyal to Evel in some ways."

"They're gonna be split up real soon," predicted Barton.

"*Very* soon," corrected Millard.

19

Night Caller

THE intern was dressed in white pants and coat and walked with a decided limp.

He came so quietly out of the darkness surrounding El Instituto de Los Malsanos that he immediately blended into the milieu and seemed a part of it.

Only fifty yards from the main entrance, he paused, cocking his head to one side. Now he looked out of place—like an interloper who feared discovery. What he heard were voices from inside the main reception area, moving toward the front door.

The intern silently stepped behind a grove of bushes, losing himself in the shadows. Two very burly men in white —male nurses of the sanitarium—came through the doors, talking casually about the difference in quality of bullfights in Mexico City and in Tijuana. They moved on around the side of the building. When their voices had faded, the intern again proceeded toward the main entrance.

The intern slipped into the corridor, hugging the wall as he silently made his way toward the nurses' station. He paused beside a phone on the wall and removed the receiver from its hook, letting it dangle in mid air. Immediately the intern could hear the dull, resonant *bzzzzzzzz* of the disembodied instrument.

At the nurses' station a squat man, dressed in a white uniform identical to the intern's, moved to the switchboard and plugged in to accommodate what he thought was an incoming call. "Hello? . . . Hello? . . ."

The intern surreptitiously worked his way past the nurses' station, inwardly chuckling to see that the ruse had worked: the squat male nurse had his back turned and was growing impatient at the lack of reply.

The intern continued along the corridor, as quiet as death.

137

When he reached a particular door he removed a slender metal instrument from his pocket and began to pick the lock.

The intern worked deftly and silently, and within moments there was a faint click. He turned the knob a fraction of an inch at a time; the door inched open.

The intern slipped into the room.

Utter darkness. Utter silence.

The intern half-turned to close the door when he felt a powerful arm sweep across his neck and begin to choke him. Feeling his breath rush out of him, the intern brought up his hands to try to pry the arm free.

The other hand of the assailant snaked around the intern's chest, patting the pockets of his blouse, searching. "I want those keys now," demanded the voice of Will Atkins.

The intern drove his elbow back, into the pit of Will's stomach. Will's arms dropped as he groaned at the impact. He staggered back, unwillingly freeing his armlock on the intern, but Will instantly recovered and raised both arms for a renewed attack.

"Will, take it easy. It's me . . . Evel."

Will froze, his arms above his head, ready to deliver a blow. He recognized Evel, but gave no sign of that recognition. His face reflected only the outrage he felt against the bizarre and abusive treatment to which he had been subjected during the past twenty-four hours. And it was apparent to Knievel that Will's ordeal had left him wary—even of an old friend obviously risking his life to help him. For Will's face also reflected intense suspicion as he studied Knievel, searching for some sign or hint of betrayal.

"Who let you in here?" whispered Will, still aware of other dangers that lurked on the opposite side of the door. "How'd you get past those . . ."

Knievel was holding up the tiny metal instrument. "You forget," whispered Knievel back, "I used to bust safes. Come on, Will, don't add me to your list of enemies."

But Will was still suspicious. "That's where we left off."

Knievel dismissed their stadium encounter. "Okay, so we had an argument over Tommy. Why not let it go at that."

Will began to pace the darkened room like a caged lion. "What'd you tell the kid about all this?"

"It's a cinch I didn't tell him you're a dope addict. That

kid's a one-man rooting section. He'd take on the Supreme Court if they knocked you."

It was obvious to Knievel that Will's ordeal had sapped much of his energy and emotions, and the knowledge of his son's faith in him only increased his anxiety.

Will turned his back on Knievel and succumbed to tears. It was the first time, Knievel realized, that he had ever seen Will cry.

After a moment, allowing Will as much time to himself as he dared under the dangerous circumstances, he stepped forward to grip Will's shoulder. "I know how you really feel about Tommy. One of these days you ought to tell him yourself."

Will's voice was muffled, weak from emotion. "I'll sure try."

"You've had a real bad time, pardner. Can you tell me what happened?"

Will turned to face Knievel. "I found some pictures in Jessie's room. I think he drugged me one night when we were at Long Beach and took some shots of the work trailer. Everything . . . up, down, sideways. Everything."

"What's that all about?"

Will shrugged. "I can't figure it, Evel. Then Cortland 'n this other guy and Jessie grabbed me. Took the photos back. They musta given me something because the next thing I knew, I was here, goin' crazy."

"Cortland? You're sure you saw Cortland?"

Will grew angry. "I'm not hallucinating, damn it!"

"Cortland . . . that means Millard must be involved. I wonder what the hell his game is?"

"I'm wondering about Ben Andrews," said Will. "I'm wondering now if there wasn't more to that robbery. With Ben dead, Millard had a clear field."

Will took Knievel's arm and led him toward the door. "What the hell're we waiting for, Evel? Let's bust outa this joint and start busting some heads."

Knievel pulled his arm free. He was thinking aloud when he said, "I'm still trying to figure out what Millard is up to."

"All I know is, he put me away."

"He didn't want you around for some reason."

"I don't get in anyone's way. All I do is check equipment. Fix the bikes."

"Bikes . . . I wonder. . . ." Knievel moved toward the door;

139

Will swung on him angrily. "You forget something?"

"What?"

"*Me!*"

"You gotta stay here, Will. If you bust out, Millard'll know we're onto his game."

Will was dismayed. "How *long* do I have to stay?"

"At least until after the jump tomorrow afternoon."

"Jump? But I have to be there . . . to check out your bikes."

"Don't sweat that detail, pardner. This is one time I'll have to go it alone."

Will surrendered, realizing, even through his semi-drugged brain, that Knievel was thinking more logically. "Okay, okay. . . . Evel?"

Knievel turned, waiting. "Yeah?"

"Take care of Tommy . . . until I can get back and do it myself."

"You bet I'll take care of Tommy."

20

Betrayal

BULLFIGHTS and sporting events at El Estadio del Sol attracted moderate to large crowds, depending on the drawing power of the Latin American personalities, but nowhere near as large as the Evel Knievel jump.

By noon the parking lot was jammed with thousands of cars, and hundreds more hopelessly clogged the arteries leading to the stadium. People also came by bicycles, ox carts, motorbikes and burros—and some came on foot from as far as fifty miles away.

Whether rich intelligentsia, middle-class workers or dirt-poor peasants, the people passing through the entrance ramps had a look of wonderment on their faces—as if they had come on this pilgrimage to bear witness to a miracle. And who was to say that Evel Knievel jumping was not in some ways miraculous?

By noon it was obvious to the personnel at the main gate that the event was a sellout—and then some. Many disappointed people would have to be turned away before the day was over.

The stadium tingled with packed humanity. The temperature was well over ninety as the people sat shoulder to shoulder, yet no one seemed troubled by the heat—curiosity and speculation were the things that increased the temperature of the people and sometimes boiled their blood.

"*Ola amigo!* You think this Evel Knievel, he will do the jump?"

"If he does not I will give him my burro. Margarita will leap over the fire gladly."

"They say that in America this wild one leaped over thirty *automoviles*."

"That is nothing, *muchacho*. They say that in England he leaped over thirty-two buses."

141

"*Carumbe.* That would be something to see."

"Thirty-two buses? Impossible. Black magic."

"It is said to be true."

"Is this Evel Knievel man or devil?"

"He is said to be a saint among children. They say he brings them gifts in the night, and then hurries away again. Papá Noel."

"He has no beard."

"*El hombre es loco.* A fall from the machine has scrambled his brains."

"*Dispensame,* señor, but if you think him so crazy, why did you walk so far to be here?"

"It was a beautiful day and there was nothing better to do. Should I sit on my porch and count the chickens in the road?"

"Pass the *pulque,* piggish one. Will you drink it all yourself?"

"If I did, I could go down there and jump myself. Without a bike."

"... *Dos pesos*? It is the bet of a fool."

"Then amuse the whim of a fool."

"No mortal man could cross such a place without falling and burning himself to a cinder."

"Who said this man Knievel was mortal? I merely said he would complete the jump and live. Come, such a small bet."

"*Muy bien. Dos pesos.* What the Americans call 'the sucker bet.' "

At one o'clock a tenseness enveloped the event. Latecomers did not walk to their seats—they rushed. Extra squads of police stood at intervals, watching for the slightest sign of disturbance, which would not be tolerated.

Vendors moved avariciously through the throngs of people who now littered the aisles and crowded the entrance ramps, craning their necks to see around heads which were also craning. The vendors were eager to sell souvenir programs and foods both indigenous and Yankee: beer, hot dogs, tacos, tortillas, burritos, hamburgers and Coca-Cola.

The arena was alive with color, movement and sound. Red-white-blue bunting, in keeping with the Knievel motif, lined the bleachers and grandstand; bright-colored pennants waved gently in the wisp of an afternoon breeze.

A traditional mariachi band marched across the field, playing the colorful tunes of Mexico. In the center of the field, stretching between the jumping and landing ramps, was a pit of fire; flames shot high in the air, as if practicing for the moment when Knievel would pass overhead. The pit was flanked by natives in Aztec headdresses, performing tribal dances, and men in asbestos suits—a grim reminder that if Knievel failed in his attempt he would have to be extracted from the hellish predicament.

The jumping ramp swept all the way up from the playing field onto the landscaped hillside north of the main grandstand. The rampway disappeared inside a wooden boxlike enclosure (referred to by its designers as the "turnaround room") twenty-four feet long and fifteen feet wide. Its sides were boarded up except for an opening in the center just wide enough to admit, or expel, a Harley-Davidson.

Flanking this opening were the seals of the United States of America and the Republic of Mexico. Bunting hung above the opening, giving the structure a stagelike appearance. Exactly the kind of showcase Knievel had insisted on, since he felt that it gave his act an extra touch of showmanship.

This tiny structure was not only a good turnaround point, but also it was adjoined by a small workshop, where Will had suggested he keep a spare jump bike, several jump suits, coveralls and tools, should any emergency repairs be necessary. Will had also suggested that once Knievel had ridden into the box, he should wait a short while, building suspense. Then streak out! That would evoke a response.

The sunlight was intensely bright and there was a roaring diversity of sounds in the packed stadium. The cacophony was a welcome enhancement to the atmosphere, adding to the tension that hung over the stadium.

In the press box Frank Gifford, dressed vividly in a red shirt and yellow blazer, went over his notes one final time for a Mexican announcer who would be translating for him. Gifford signaled that he was ready to go and stared into the lens of an XHWB-TV camera.

Buenos tardes, *ladies and gentlemen. That's good afternoon down here south of the border. We're talking to you from El Estadio del Sol, the Stadium of the Sun, and as you've already seen on your TV screens, it's fiesta time in Mexico today. This vibrant, excited, thrill-seeking crowd has turned out by the thousands for one of its greatest idols ... Evel Knievel.*

A parade flowed onto the field, led by a troop of horsemen carrying the U.S. and Mexican flags and riding prancing, spirited animals. Following the stallions came a kaleidoscope of color in the form of three phalanxes of youngsters on bicycles. Next came the mariachi band and then Knievel's entire mobile inventory: trucks, vans, the Stutz, the Cadillac pick-up, the Snake River rocket.

Well, ladies and gentlemen, they love a parade the world over and as you can see, here it comes. It's led by Mexican caballeros riding the finest horses the country has to offer. Listen to that music. That's a mariachi band. And look at those kids on their bikes. And there's Evel's trucks and vans bringing up the rear. We're seeing the biggest invasion of Mexico since Cortez arrived . . . but this one is peaceful.

In the thirty-foot-wide vehicle tunnel at the southern end of the stadium, where the Knievel caravan had parked following the parade, Kate seemed a different woman—serious, withdrawn—as she placed a telephoto lens onto the Nikon draped around her neck on a strap. Standing next to the equipment van were two bikes: one for wheelies, one for the actual jump. A few feet away, at a phone booth, Tommy held the receiver against his ear, a frightened, desolate, unhappy child, whose appearance seemed pitiable to Kate as the boy fought back tears. ". . . but . . . but . . . when *can* I see my father?"

The voice of Thompson, the "resident administrator," came sternly over the wire—lacking even the faintest suggestion of bedside manner. "Well, I'm afraid you'll have to be patient. First he's got to regain his strength."

Desperation invaded Tommy's voice. "Can I please talk to him?"

The voice coming over the wire remained unmoved. "Sorry, that's out of the question. He's undergone a terrible ordeal."

Tommy refused to give up or hang up; he clutched the receiver as though it were a life preserver. "Can't I just say hello?"

"Next week perhaps . . ." Vague, unreassuring.

"Would . . . would you please give him a message for me?"

"Certainly." Hesitant, unreassuring.

"Just say . . . tell him I love him."

"Very well." Indifferent, unreassuring.

It was Thompson who hung up; Tommy was still holding the receiver when Kate walked to him and placed it back in its cradle. "They won't let you see him?"

Tommy nodded, fighting back the tears.

"Did you find out *anything*?" asked Kate.

"Nope."

Knievel emerged from his recreational van, resplendent in a blue jump suit with the standard red-white-blue Knievel motif and a waistband with a huge buckle enscribed with the initials EK. He put the finishing adjustments to his billowing blue cape and saw the expression on Tommy's face. He didn't have to be told what the boy was experiencing.

"They won't let Tommy see Will," said Kate.

Knievel checked the handlebars of his wheelie bike. "They wouldn't let me see him either. But I did. Last night."

Tommy whirled, coming alive again. "You did? How is he?"

"Don't worry, Tommy," said Knievel reassuringly. "He's going to be okay. And as soon as this jump is over, I'm going to pay another visit to that sanitarium. I'm gonna get him out of there."

"How?" asked Tommy wide-eyed.

"You're going to have to let me worry about that. In the meantime, don't you worry about him, Tommy." Knievel rumpled Tommy's hair and turned to get on his wheelie bike. The boy looked at Kate, wanting her endorsement as proof that he'd see his father soon. Kate gave that endorsement, even though she was preoccupied. She told Tommy to wait by the van while she hurried to Knievel's side.

"Evel," said Kate, "I want you to know something."

Knievel had climbed onto the wheelie bike and was ready to go. "What is it, Kate?"

"All of a sudden, I hate my assignment."

"Why?"

"I don't want to shoot your last jump. I don't want you to *have* a last jump. Ever."

"That's about the best news I've had since I started riding. And it's the nicest thing you've said to me since I first met you."

"Just be careful," warned Kate. "Take care of yourself."

"I'll do that," promised Knievel. "Because now I've got a special reason."

He kicked the Harley alive and roared onto the field, waving at Tommy. Kate signaled for the boy to join her and she slid her arm around his shoulder.

"Is he gonna be all right?" wondered Tommy.

"He's gonna be better than he's ever been before," said Kate, fighting back a tear.

Ladies and gentlemen, I've never felt anything like this before. There's electricity in the air here at Estadio del Sol. Because this is Evel Knievel's first appearance in Mexico, and the crowd is wild with anticipation.

. . . That isn't a barbecue pit in the center of the stadium . . . that's a certain death trap if Evel Knievel fails to clear it when he jumps in just a short while.

There was deafening applause when Knievel rode onto the field. He raised one hand from the handlebars to acknowledge the thunderous homage. The crowd rose to its feet as a single unit, giving their daredevil hero an ear-splitting welcome.

This audience has just gone wild, ladies and gentlemen. And now Evel is going to ride up to the announcer positioned in the center of the stadium and say a few words for us.

Knievel took the microphone and studied the packed grandstands. Audience turnout was something that had never ceased to startle him and put a lump in his throat, even if he publicly refused to admit it.

"Folks," said Knievel into the microphone, "this is a big honor for me." He paused while the announcer translated into Spanish. Wild, enthusiastic applause.

"Our two countries are sister nations. That makes us all relatives." Translation. Again, unrestrained applause. Knievel had to wait a full minute before it was quiet enough for him to continue. "I'm proud to try for a new world's record here today." He handed the microphone back as the announcer finished the translation.

The crowd's reception was even infectious to Gifford, who considered himself a jaded professional.

Ladies and gentlemen, Evel Knievel has already turned this crowd into a personal cheering section today. Well, he'll need all the good wishes he can get. Because he's jumping over one hundred and sixty feet of flaming, burning, blazing fire. A mistake now could cost Evel Knievel his life.

As Knievel performed his warm-up wheelies for the cheering throngs, Barton poked his head through the rear doors of the ambulance parked near the southern vehicle tunnel. He was dressed in white and held in his hands a radio transmitter. Satisfied to see Knievel on the field, he returned to the front seat and pressed a mobile headphone to his ear. "Barton here," he said in a low voice.

In a private box next to the battery of sports reporters, radio and TV newsmen, sat Millard, Cortland and Clark. Millard had the phone next to his ear. "Are you ready on your end?"

Barton's voice: "Ready and waiting."

"Good." Millard set the telephone receiver back on its cradle and glanced at Cortland. "Barton is set."

"Why doesn't Knievel get on with it and make the run?" asked Cortland nervously. "What's he waiting for?"

"Relax," said Millard. "It's all part of the act. Pretty soon he'll get his jump bike. But the countdown doesn't start until he's up there . . . at the top of the ramp."

That fire you've just seen is over one hundred and sixty feet of flaming death. Evel's going to jump it wearing only his ordinary leathers. He must clear that fiery pit. Hang on, ladies and gentlemen, for the thrill of your life.

Finished performing his spectacular wheelies, Knievel returned to the vehicle tunnel, where Kate and Tommy were waiting for him. Knievel shut down the bike, dismounted and took off his helmet.

"Those were great wheelies," said Tommy.

"Thanks, Tommy. That baby ready to go?" he asked, indicating the jump bike.

"Sure is."

Knievel grinned. "Well, time to get this show on the road. Can't keep the customers waiting any longer." He gave Kate a friendly smile and tousled Tommy's hair as he climbed aboard the jump bike. "Time to go for broke." He started the cycle. Kate raised both hands: each middle finger was crossed over the forefinger.

"Hey, don't forget your helmet," said Tommy.

Knievel took the crash helmet from Tommy and slapped it down onto his head. "Thanks, pardner. I see you haven't forgotten a thing I taught you."

And he was off.

To perform another jump.

Kate's hands were still in the air.

For good luck.

Evel Knievel has just ridden onto the field aboard his jump bike, ladies and gentlemen. It won't be long now. Down here in Mexico, macho . . . or machismo . . . is a very important word. It means bravery and courage. It also means daring and the display of a man's honor. Well, today this Mexi-

147

can audience is here to salute a man who has proven he has macho *all over the world . . . Evel Knievel.*

As Knievel performed another wheelie around the edges of the stadium, allowing crowds one last close-up glimpse, pressure was mounting in Millard's box.

Cortland's nerves were showing as he turned to Millard. "I'm worried," he said.

"What about?"

"Jessie."

"All right, Gunther. Get it off your chest. What about Jessie?"

"We're in Mexico and we've got Evel. Thanks to Jessie. But he's a junkie . . ."

At that very moment, Jessie was approaching the box. He overheard Cortland. He paused behind a pillar, out of sight of the others.

". . . and I don't trust junkies. He's on a high right now. Meanwhile, you promised to make him number one jumper. The two things don't go together. I say we get rid of Jessie."

Jessie listened, not moving.

"Rest easy, Gunther," said Millard. "Don't take me for such a fool. Jessie is finished. Norman is going to see to that personally. Aren't you, Norman?"

Clark patted his bulging breast pocket. "As personally as I can make it, Mr. Millard."

"See, Gunther? You've got nothing to worry about. Now settle back and enjoy the show. You're about to be royally entertained."

Jessie turned silently and moved backwards several feet, still unobserved by the three men, whose attention was riveted on the playing field. Then he turned and hurried off.

Jessie elbowed his way past a cameraman, upsetting the man's sound cables but ignoring his cries of protest. On Jessie's face was an injured albeit determined look. Maybe Norman Clark would have his "personal" satisfaction, but not before Jessie had enjoyed one final ride.

Which would prove to the world that he, not Evel Knievel, was *numero uno.*

I've watched Evel Knievel jump more times than I can remember, ladies and gentlemen. But I've never become accustomed to the danger. Death is always riding with Evel. He's the only one who can laugh at death.

Finished with the wheelies, Knievel started up the jump ramp, disappearing into the turnaround booth. The cheering suddenly died down and twenty thousand throats became simultaneously dry.

A minute ticked away. Suddenly the Harley shot out of the boxed enclosure, streaking along the ramp. And just as suddenly, a gasp escaped from twenty thousand throats.

Smoke burned from the rear wheel of the Harley as Knievel came to an abrupt stop two-thirds of the way up the jump ramp.

Kate's hand went to her mouth. Tommy watched with clenched fists. The gallery gasped again, a mixture of disappointment and surprise. Knievel backed the Harley to the ground, then zoomed across the field, picking up speed.

Evel didn't like something about that approach, ladies and gentlemen. Now he's returning to the ramp to the turn-around room, where he'll kick off a second attempt. These things are not uncommon. Evel has a built-in instinct during a jump, and if he suspects he isn't moving at the proper speed, or the bike doesn't feel right to him, he'll abort, go back and try again.

21

Jessie's Ride to Glory

KNIEVEL had just positioned his bike in the turnaround room and was revving the engine for his second attempt when Jessie came through the door that led to the spare-parts chamber.

He was grasping his crash helmet, his face taut with tension. Jessie's life hung in the balance, and he knew it.

"Off the bike, Evel."

Knievel was startled. "What the hell'd you say?"

"End of the line, man."

Knievel recomposed himself with his usual aplomb. "What're you talking about? You're supposed to be at the other end, not here."

Jessie's excitement was unrestrained. "Always have been before. But not any longer. Now it's my turn, man. My shot at the glory. Get off that bike. I'm making this jump."

"What the hell's got into you, Jessie? That crowd paid their pesos to see me jump, not you."

"No way, man. *I'm* jumping. I always knew I was better'n you and today I'm going to prove it. Now you just get outta my way."

"Hey, you been smokin' something? You're high."

"Man," shouted Jessie, becoming more volatile. "Maybe you oughta get high. So you'll know what's really going on. Hey, Millard wants to kill you. And your buddy Will too. You know, he thinks he's even gonna kill me."

"Why? Why would Millard do that?"

"Man, Millard only brought you down here for one purpose—and that's so he could take your body back to the States as cover for about fifty million bucks of cocaine. Now get out of my way."

Knievel revved the Harley, studying the ramp that led from the turnaround room. "Look, Jessie, we'll straighten all that out later. Right now I've got a jump—"

Knievel never saw Jessie's hand descending toward his neck. There was an instant of pain and then blackness.

Jessie lifted the slumping Knievel from the Harley and placed him gently on the floor. Then he hurried into the spare-parts room, where several spare sets of Knievel's leathers hung from hooks. He took down a pair that matched what Knievel was wearing. As he changed, he draped his own clothing over the Strato-Cycle.

The Strato-Cycle . . . that would be the bike he'd make all his future jumps on, he decided, right then and there. It would become his own personal trademark . . . the bike of tomorrow ridden by the star of today. *Numero uno.*

I've never seen Evel Knievel take this much time before a jump. He must be sizing up that ramp very carefully, ladies and gentlemen. It could be there's something out of alignment on the ramp, or it could be the bike itself. It's not uncommon for Evel to change bikes moments before a jump if something doesn't feel proper about it. It's a sixth sense he's developed. . . .

Reactions to the delay were taking place all over El Estadio del Sol. Cortland shifted as nervously and as frequently as a Mexican jumping bean. "Now what's the holdup?"

"Relax," said a relaxed Millard. "Just take it easy. Like I said, Evel'll jump but at his own pace."

Kate: "Something's wrong."

Tommy: "He promised to be careful. Maybe he's doing like Mr. Gifford said. Checking the bike."

In the turnaround room, Jessie emerged from the spare-parts chamber, now dressed identically to Knievel, down to the billowing blue cape. As he buttoned his helmet strap, he glanced down at his old jumping companion. "So long . . . ex-champ."

And he zoomed out to glory.

Here he comes, ladies and gentlemen . . . Evel Knievel. Riding toward triumph or tragedy.

The Harley swooped down the jump ramp and climbed again, streaking toward the leap-off point. The Mexican crowd rose as a single body, its shriek a deafening sound.

The motorcycle departed the jump ramp at ninety-two miles per hour and sailed gracefully above the blazing pit of fire. The natives in headdresses and the men in asbestos suits

152

craned to watch the winged man soaring above them.

In a fraction of a second, Frank Gifford foresaw that the bike was going to land perfectly. He had reported too many Knievel jumps not to know when it was going beautifully. And this was going to be one of the most beautiful jumps he had ever witnessed.

He was all ready to make his next comment when the bike touched down, exactly as he had foreseen.

But there was something he hadn't foreseen.

The front tire blew.

It was flattened in a second and the bike was completely out of control.

And so was its rider.

He was plucked off the seat by the invisible fingers of momentum and flung through space with the thrust of a jet rocket and the resistance of a rag doll. His arms and legs flailed against the propulsion without noticeable effect.

There was something incongruous about those gyrating arms and legs, and the general shape of the hurtling body, that struck Gifford as being out of proportion to the Evel Knievel he knew so well.

But he had no time to contemplate some intangible uncertainty as he realized the immense danger Knievel was in.

Oh my God. As you can see on your television screens, this may be the worst of the Evel Knievel crashes.

It was. The body, twisted and turning limply, scraped across the surface of the landing ramp with a grating sound that sickened the stomachs of those close enough to hear it. Several snapping noises were also heard by those on the fringe of the fire trench.

The impact was so great that the crash helmet leaped from the rider's head, as though it had a life-force of its own, and spiraled toward the grandstand. Gifford instinctively knew this was a bad sign. A broken neck for certain. Broken spine? Very probable, if not certain.

The awful thing that happened next brought a fresh gasp from the Mexican stadium. The handlebars of the Harley lashed out like some angry beast and rolled across the top of the biker's unprotected head. Gifford winced. Crushed skull . . . no uncertainty about that.

Millard, Cortland and Clark watched from their private box as though they were at a Saturday matinee enjoying a Western.

"Barton was right on the button," chuckled Cortland.

"I told you there was nothing to worry about," said Millard.

"Very nice, Mr. Millard," added Clark. "Without a doubt, that was Evel's greatest jump."

Kate and Tommy watched the rolling body in stunned silence—unable to speak, to move, to think. Their blood was cold with horror, their minds numb with shock.

Collectively, the spectators were under the spell of a phenomenon. Since the sound of the exploding tire, and the realization of impending disaster, silence had fallen over the stadium, broken only by the unified gasps. It seemed that except for the horribly twisted body of the jumper, toppling head over heels, El Estadio del Sol was in a state of suspended animation.

Man and machine came to a stop forty yards from the end of the touch-down ramp. Only the cycle moved as its befouled engine still tried to force the broken machine ahead.

Barton and another ambulance attendant were the first to reach the prostrate body. Barton rolled it over and found himself staring into wide-open, lifeless eyes, as he had expected to do.

But they were Jessie Hammond's—not Evel Knievel's. For ten full seconds Barton was unable to do anything but stare back into the accusing eyes.

The medics have reached him now. They're putting Evel on a stretcher. I pray to God they get him to the hospital in time. This looks very bad, ladies and gentlemen, very bad.

As the other attendants loaded the corpse into the back of the ambulance, Barton hurried to the front seat and called Millard.

"Barton? Nice work."

"Save it."

"He's dead, isn't he?"

"He's dead, all right, but it's not Knievel."

"What the hell—?"

"It's Jessie. Jessie Hammond."

In the private box, gloating and back-slapping had been short-lived. Millard slammed down the phone, his body trembling. Cortland was shaken—he had never seen Millard lose control like this before.

Finally Millard seemed to be in control of his emotions again and wiped a speck of lint from the seat in front of him

—a sign to Cortland that Millard was thinking, and thinking fast.

"What happened?" asked Cortland, almost reluctantly.

"Listen carefully. Take Jessie's body to the hacienda. I'll get a death certificate in Evel's name and meet you there. We'll switch trailers at the hacienda as planned and start for the States this afternoon. It'll still be Evel Knievel's funeral procession crossing the border. And we'll still get waved through."

"What do you mean, take *Jessie's body?* That's supposed to be Knievel down there."

"Supposed to be, but isn't," said Millard.

"What went wrong?" asked Cortland.

"It's Jessie who's dead. Not Knievel."

"How'd that happen?" asked Clark.

"How the hell do I know."

"Maybe Jessie blew the whole thing to Knievel."

"A very good maybe. We'd better get to Knievel before he gets to the cops."

Clark smiled and started for the door.

"Norman," said Millard. "Stop him *cold.*"

Clark smiled again, nodded his head and left.

Millard turned to Cortland: "You get down there and grab Will's kid and that photographer dame with him. Just in case we need more leverage."

Cortland twisted anxiously. Abducting people was something a little out of his line. But he could detect by the urgency in Millard's voice that he had better perform, and perform well, if he wanted to see the caper carried to its successful completion. He reminded himself of the fifty million dollars waiting for them on the other side of the border.

It was all the motive Cortland needed.

On the field, the ambulance moved toward the vehicle tunnel. The sound of the siren diminished and faded. The stadium remained wrapped in a strange, deathlike hush. Fans stood, immobilized into muteness out of respect for the fallen biker.

In the turnaround room, Knievel popped into consciousness as suddenly as unconsciousness had engulfed him. He pushed himself erect, the top of his head throbbing painfully enough to make him stagger.

He slammed against the wall, feeling the effects of a hangover—only this was a blackjack hangover, he told himself, remembering the incident with Jessie.

155

Knievel stumbled to the opening just in time to hear Frank Gifford recap the accident, and affirm the likelihood of serious injuries, if not death. So, thought Knievel, Jessie hadn't found the glory he so desperately sought.

But what of Millard and his plan to ship Knievel's body back to the States? That could still work if Jessie died and it was never announced that Knievel had not taken the ride. (And judging from the way Gifford talked, everyone still thought it was Evel on the way to the hospital.)

Right now he needed Will, who was the only help he could really count on. Unfortunately, there wouldn't be time to explain to the police or anyone else who hadn't been exposed to some phase of Millard's plot to smuggle cocaine across the border. His immediate plan was to get Will out of the sanitarium and play it by ear after that.

Knievel lurched into the spare-parts chamber, the pain in the top of his head suddenly forgotten when he saw the Strato-Cycle for the first time and was captivated by its audacious wing-swept design. He wondered who had created it.

It looked like an Evel Knievel machine, even though he had nothing to do with it. He would have to incorporate it into his caravan—make it part of each show. Perhaps do his wheelies on it, instead of a standard Harley-Davidson. Still, he wondered . . .

Was this futuristic bike part of the scheme between Millard and Jessie? Had the bike been a form of bribery to bring Jessie into the plan, with additional promises of untold riches and fame as a jumper?

There wasn't time for further speculation. He climbed out of his jump leathers, donning a pair of orange coveralls. He turned and headed for the only exit door from the boxlike structure when he saw Norman Clark, a pistol in his hand, approaching. Knievel ducked behind the door and waited. Millard must have found out it was Jessie on the bike and had sent Clark to make sure Knievel hadn't learned more than he should. That part of it was obvious.

After a moment the door opened slowly and Clark entered, his attention on the panel that led to the main chamber. Knievel stepped out, his arm moving swiftly downward to deliver a vicious karate chop to the back of Clark's neck. The gunsel crumpled to the plank flooring.

Knievel bent down and retrieved the fallen pistol, a snubnosed .32, shoved it into a pocket of his coveralls and pushed the Strato-Cycle out through the rear door.

156

Slapping on a crash helmet, he kicked the jet bike to life, startled by the amount of power he could feel throbbing against his legs. Slowly, in order to adapt himself to the bike's powerful thrust, he built up speed, permeated with the sensation of propulsion he had only experienced at Snake River.

After only a minute he realized that he could easily kill or maim himself on this fantastic cycle, and he continued to exercise wariness by testing the braking system, checking the steering and getting the "feel" of it—just as he would have done with any unfamiliar machine.

Finally feeling some sense of competence with the bike, he streaked down the landscaped hillside and passed the parking lot, his body hunched over and totally unrecognizable to passersby.

At that moment, as the Strato-Cycle passed from sight of the stadium, Kate and Tommy were walking through the reserved-parking area. Kate tried to comfort the boy. "Evel's had worse smash-ups, Tommy." She knew she was lying to herself *and* Tommy but she couldn't bring herself to tell the truth.

"There's been trouble ever since I came," said Tommy. "I'm just bad luck. For everyone."

"Stop that," insisted Kate. "There's no such thing as someone *being* bad luck."

But Tommy was ignoring her, lost in his own guilt, and perhaps sensing that Kate was hiding the truth from him. "First my dad, now Evel."

Kate faced Tommy, bending forward until they were only inches apart. "Tommy, you've got to stop thinking this way. You're the most wonderful boy in the world. Didn't anyone ever tell you that?"

In a low voice, Tommy answered, "I never had anyone . . ."

Kate took his hand, holding on tightly. "You have now."

As they passed between two cars to reach Kate's Cadillac convertible, they saw Cortland standing in their path, as if he had been waiting for them.

Kate felt a sense of relief. Millard must have sent Cortland to comfort them until official word of Evel's condition. Yet he had a pained expression on his face that bothered Kate. He said pleasantly, "I wouldn't let you fight this traffic." And took a step forward . . .

22

Crash Out

EL Instituto de los Malsanos sweltered under the mid-afternoon sun. Because the air-conditioning system had broken down at dawn and repairmen would not be available until the following day, the staff and patients had suffered throughout the day.

Thompson was feeling the effects of the irritating heat—indolence, ennui, thirst—when he was called to the nurses' station and handed the phone by one of the male nurses.

"Yes?" he asked, wiping the sweat from his forehead with a towel the nurse also handed him.

"This is Millard." Cold, hard, urgent.

His suffering was forgotten for the moment. "Why yes, Mr. Millard," he said, feigning formality.

"I'm calling in regard to a certain patient."

Thompson nodded. "Yes, I understand."

"I want that patient in solitary to have the *most complete* treatment you can give him."

Thompson studied a spider building its web in a corner of the wall. "I'll handle it. Personally. You can dismiss the patient from your mind."

Thompson was still studying the spider's techniques, and had yet to return the phone to the male nurse, when the Strato-Cycle crashed through the sanitarium doors.

Wood, plaster and shattered glass were suddenly dangerous missiles hurtling toward Thompson—but not half as deadly as the man piloting the Strato-Cycle.

Thompson instinctively shielded his face from the flying particles and desperately hugged the wall as the Strato-Cycle bounded past him. He was aware that this was no ordinary motorcycle—it had to be driven by a madman! He turned in time to catch a glimpse of the rider's grimly determined face and knew he would need all the help he could muster.

"Charlie! Tom!" he cried into the nurses' station. "On the double."

By then Knievel had already stopped the Strato-Cycle before the door of Will's room. "Will!" he shouted. "Get away against the wall. I'm going to blow this goddamn lock off!"

Knievel leveled the snub-nosed .32 and fired twice. The slugs splintered the lock and the wood around it. Will flung open the door and lumbered out, still dazed by the drug, but hurrying as best he could. "Come on, old man," yelled Knievel, "get a move on. There's a reception committee right behind me."

Will climbed laboriously onto the back of the Strato-Cycle, and Knievel turned it back down the corridor.

He aimed it like a gun.

Just in time to face Thompson and his two burliest guards, Charlie and Tom. But Charlie and Tom, and even Thompson, who had thousands riding on the outcome of Millard's caper, realized there was no way in their power to stop the killer motorcycle as it jetted toward them. They did the only smart thing: they flung themselves against the walls of the corridor.

The bike zoomed past.

After that, Thompson decided there were some things no amount of money could force a man to do and decided to let the matter drop. Charlie and Tom had similar sentiments.

The Strato-Cycle roared like a charging monster past the shattered doors, jolted down the stairs and swung onto the main road.

Will was hanging on for dear life as he shouted, "How's the boy?"

"Great," Knievel shouted back. "Except for being worried about you."

"Where is Tommy?" asked Will. The fresh air streaming past his face had the effect of smelling salts, clearing away the maze of cobwebs which had turned his thinking fuzzy for the past two days.

"Probably back at the hacienda by now," guessed Knievel.

"Then get a move on," laughed Will. "So he can stop worrying about his old man."

23

Switch

THE Mexican Tourist Bureau would never have condoned what was happening at Rancho Vista Hermosa.

The ambulance that had carried the body from the stadium was parked in front of the deserted reception office, its two regular attendants bound and gagged and stuffed away in the back, forgotten for the moment. Flanking the ambulance were two tractor-trailer rigs side by side.

The dimensions of the two trucks, and the make of the cabs, were identical. One belonged to Evel Knievel: it was his equipment van. The other carried the lettering of a Mexican grocery chain: this was the rig Barton had driven from up north.

Clark and Barton, with the help of two laborers, were in the process of removing the outer panels of the "grocery" van and stacking them against the wall. As each piece came away, it became apparent that the new skin beneath was an exact re-creation of the exterior of Knievel's van—lettering, colors, everything.

In another few minutes the duplicate truck had shed its metal skin, and Evel's van was ready to be cloaked in it.

The switch was almost complete—all it needed now were the finishing touches.

Nearby, watching impatiently though smugly, were Millard and Cortland. The roof of the Porsche had been removed, so there were only the windshield and roll bar remaining. Millard's nervousness was counterbalanced by his knowledge that hidden behind the exterior metal wall were three thousand bags of cocaine. Worth millions on the drug market.

He strode toward the duplicate truck, where Barton was sliding the first panel into place over Knievel's rig. "Will you hurry it up, Barton."

"Won't take five minutes," he promised.

"Good," said Millard, rubbing his hands together. "Now, bring Jessie out."

"Right you are."

Knievel had switched off the Strato-Cycle, much to Will's objections, several hundred yards from the hacienda for fear the roar of the jet engine might attract unwanted attention.

With Will muttering under his breath, impatient to rejoin his son, they worked their way quietly through a grove of trees, stopping on the fringe and crouching down to see Barton placing the "grocery" panels over Knievel's rig.

"I'm seeing double," said Will, bewildered. "What the hell is Millard doing?"

"Let's watch and see," suggested Knievel.

A moment later the two laborers and Norman Clark carried a coffin from the ambulance and placed it inside the duplicate trailer.

Knievel dared only whisper. "Jessie said they were gonna try to knock me off so they'd take my body back to the States in the van. Only it's a fake van. Loaded with dope. It all makes sense now."

"Doesn't make any sense to me," growled Will.

"Remind me to tell you about it sometime," said Knievel.

Barton finished covering Knievel's equipment van with the "grocery" panels and immediately went to work sliding panels onto the dummy rig. In minutes it was an exact match of the equipment truck. When the switch was completed, Millard called into the house. "Come on, come on. Let's get going."

Cortland and Clark came through an archway of the hacienda, pushing Kate and Tommy ahead of them at gunpoint.

When Will saw his son, it took all of Knievel's strength to prevent him from rushing from behind the trees.

"Tommy . . ."

"Hold it, Will. Hold it, damn it. It's six guns against one. And we need those bikes." He gestured to the pair of Harleys parked next to the duplicate van. "We've got to lower the odds or we don't stand a chance."

Cortland was in high spirits as he helped Barton load Kate and Tommy into the back of the duplicate van. "Perfect," he congratulated Millard. "Building this duplicate to hide the cocaine in was worth all the trouble and expense. It's just the way you laid it out that night at your home six months ago."

Millard chuckled. "I had help. Now let's move the merchandise across the border." Millard turned to one of the laborers. "When we leave, you take Knievel's rig out into the desert somewhere. Somewhere far away. And ditch it. Then meet us in Texas as planned."

Barton and Clark climbed into the cab of the duplicate truck while Cortland joined Millard in the Porsche.

Knievel and Will remained hidden as the two vehicles—the so-called funeral cortege—drove past them, headed for the main highway. "Now," said Knievel, "let's help ourselves to those bikes."

It took only a minute for Knievel and Will to get the drop on the two laborers, whom they locked in the back of Knievel's "grocery" van. Securing the door, Knievel pointed to the bikes. "That's all we need, Will."

But the ex-jumper didn't have to be told. He had already put on the helmet that had been draped over the handlebars and was kicking the bike to life. Knievel joined him and within thirty seconds they had left the hacienda behind.

24

Pursuit

ON Highway 45, driving the Porsche northward, Millard had a confident, almost contented, look. As usual, Cortland was tense, afraid to take anything for granted. It looked to him as if they had pulled it off successfully, but because he was the eternal pessimist, he thought back over recent events, searching for holes they might have forgotten to plug up.

One thing that bothered Cortland was Norman Clark. He had returned untriumphant from his search for Knievel with a lump on his neck, a monumental headache and a report that had made Cortland's heart leap into his throat. Knievel remained unkillable and very much loose—but where? Why hadn't he made an attempt to stop them at the hacienda if Jessie had revealed the plan to him? Cortland decided to convey his fears to Millard, whose look of confidence would not be dispelled.

"What do you think Knievel will do?" asked Cortland.

"When he can't find Kate and Tommy, he'll be looking for us. That's what I'm counting on. We'll finish him once and for all."

Ahead of the Porsche was the duplicate rig, which took the corners dangerously fast, Clark at the wheel, Barton beside him.

Inside the trailer, Kate and Tommy braced themselves against a wall and dodged tools and spare parts that kept falling from the racks as Clark sped around the curves.

Kate kissed Tommy lightly on the top of his head, trying to ease his fears. "You can't quit now, Tommy. You're the man on this team. And I need your help."

Far enough behind the Porsche so that neither Cortland nor Millard could see them were the two motorcycles.

Knievel pointed to his right and veered off across the highway to speed onto a dirt road running parallel to the main thoroughfare. Will followed.

When the parallel dirt road was no more, Knievel angled his bike up a steep hillside—again Will followed unquestioningly.

When they reached the top, the two bikes drew parallel and stopped, watching the caravan as it continued down the highway.

Knievel turned to Will. "I'll let the Porsche see me and draw them off. That way there's a chance for you to surprise the guys in the truck."

Will's voice was hoarse. "Right plan . . . wrong players." He jabbed a finger against his chest. "*I'll* take the Porsche."

"Yeah," said Knievel, "and you'll be good as dead. There's nobody Millard would rather see dead right now."

"I know that," said Will. "What choice do I have? I'm too old. I wouldn't stand a chance against those two goons in the rig."

Knievel thought it over, then handed Will the snub-nosed .32 pistol. "All right, Will. Take this. It'll help even the odds."

Will gunned the engine of the cycle but delayed his take-off to tell Knievel: "Save my kid, pardner." Then Will shot forward, working his way skillfully through precipitous terrain. It was good dirt-riding for a guy who hadn't been on a bike in a long time and who had been hitting the bottle pretty hard for the last few years. Knievel would have to congratulate him when this whole mess was cleaned up.

Will continued his perilous ride down the slope toward the highway, kicking up dust, scattering pebbles and rocks and refusing to flinch as his insides were shaken up by the wild ride.

Will felt the thirst growing within him but he fought against the urge. Fighting the thirst would have to take precedent in the days ahead if he were going to have any kind of new life with Tommy. In fact, there would have to be numerous changes in his attitudes and life style.

Will's motorcycle emerged on the highway within view of the Porsche. He leaned into the turn instead of steering into it, knowing that the wheels would travel in a straighter line because the centrifugal force was counterbalanced by the downward pull of gravity.

He straightened out the bike and opened up full throttle.

He gained on the navy blue Porsche as he pulled the .32 from his pocket. He couldn't remember the last time he had fired a shot, and then it hadn't been in anger. That much Will could remember, for he had never fired a gun in anger in his life. It was an unsettling sensation, the taking of a fellow human's life, and he felt his mouth turning to cotton as he brought up the revolver. Hell, it was them or Tommy.

He fired one shot.

Will's hesitancy and nervousness had not affected his marksmanship. The bullet shattered the Porsche's rear window. Glass fragments showered on Millard and Cortland, who instinctively ducked down into the seat. Cortland, who cursed himself for bad luck, cast a look into the rear-view mirror. "Jesus," he shouted, "there's someone behind us on a bike."

"Can you see who it is?" asked Cortland, shouting above the rush of wind.

"Knievel. It must be Knievel."

Millard studied his side mirror. "Knievel, hell," he cried out, "that's Will Atkins. Grab the gun in the jockey box, Gunther. Drop him. Kill him."

It was a command Cortland hated—he hadn't figured on committing murder himself. For Barton or Clark to pull the trigger—that was one thing, but *he* was a lawyer. Still, he couldn't forget the fifty million waiting in the States. He reached into the glove compartment to find a Sterling .380 double-action Model 400 with extra clips.

Cortland stood up through the open roof and snapped off a shot too hastily.

Will zigzagged the bike, almost dropping the .32 as he clutched the handlebars. He continued to weave from one side of the road to the other, presenting an elusive target. Will sat far back on the seat, hunched over in order to cut down wind resistance.

Millard saw that the shot had missed. "Hang on," he warned Cortland. "We're going after him." As the Porsche came to an intersecting dirt road, Millard went into a hard slide, twisting the wheel so that the car came around in a hundred-and-eighty-degree turn.

Will saw the Porsche facing him and, bracing himself with one dangling foot, also went into a hard slide. Before he had time to think (the action had been all reflex from his many years as a topnotch cyclist), he was headed back down

167

the highway, the Porsche now pursuing him.

Fortunes of the cat-and-mouse game.

"Kill him! Kill him!" demanded Millard in blind fury, pushing the Porsche to maximum speed.

Cortland, who had never distinguished himself as a marksman, and who found the Sterling .380 unfamiliar and therefore difficult to fire, continued to squeeze off an occasional shot, but Will also continued his evasive weaving pattern. Hitting such a moving target seemed impossible to Cortland, who was becoming more frustrated with the Sterling each time he fired it.

From his perch on the ridge, Knievel saw Will and the Porsche returning. After they had streaked past his position, he accelerated the bike and continued to follow the ridge line in the opposite direction.

Will was on his own now as Knievel went after the rig.

Will could sense the Porsche making minor gains on him and, fearful that Cortland might get lucky with his not-so-sharp-shooting, he decided it was time to get off the main highway. No use endangering the innocent lives of motorists.

Will chose a dirt road which led straight into the foothills and swerved off to follow it. He was surprised when the Porsche turned off in the same place and pursued, also without losing any speed. Will had to grudgingly admire Millard's driving: the Porsche was matching the bike, action for action.

Cortland was still in a standing position, trying for a snap shot at Atkins, but it was fruitless. Not only was the motorcycle appearing and disappearing from sight as it clung to the hilly terrain, but the Porsche was passing through chuckholes and depressions that severely jarred Cortland and sent the muzzle of the Sterling .380 all over creation.

Then the Porsche hit a smooth upgrade and the jarring leveled off. Cortland could hold the pistol steady now, and he urged Millard to stay on an even course, for Will was nearing the top of the ridge and was moving on a straight line away from the Porsche—almost like a non-moving target. And if he could catch Will silhouetted against the sky . . .

Will, meanwhile, was taking everything the Harley would give him as he neared the top of the ridge. Instinct told him to begin a slowdown and brake near the top to check the opposite slope of the ridge, but Will fought the impulse, even though he didn't have the foggiest notion what lay ahead.

As he continued through waterholes, over rocks, zig-zagging past the worst boulders, he stood up on the pegs so that the machine could be moved independently of his body. In this manner he could negotiate the obstacles either by handlebars or by the shifting of his weight. He downshifted to gain additional power—he knew that feeding more gas in a high gear would only put unnecessary strain on the engine.

His serpentine trail led him through underbrush, willows and scrub oak. The ridge line was coming up fast. A glance over his shoulder told him the Porsche was pursuing with an incredible vindictiveness, losing no speed despite the rugged terrain.

Will wondered how long the small automobile—hardly de-signed for mountain climbing—could withstand the punish-ment. He cursed the Porsche, for it had taken on the personification of its driver—it was an evil, ugly, unstoppable monster scrambling up the hillside, eager to devour him.

The image of Tommy locked in the back of the van with an equally vulnerable Kate Morgan filled him with rage, and he considered turning and racing straight for the Porsche—but it would be a losing proposition, a waste of his life.

At least this way, maintaining the role of the pursued, he had some modicum of chance—maybe the other side of the hill would slope gradually enough so that he could ride it out. And maybe Millard would think twice about sending the Porsche into what might look like a bottomless canyon.

Will heard Cortland fire again, but he wasn't too wor-ried, not with the hillside so pitted and precipitous. The odds of Cortland hitting anything under those shaky conditions were minimal.

But not minimal enough, as Will was to find out.

For Cortland fired again, just as the motorcycle reached the level of the ridge and Will was outlined against the blue, cloudless horizon.

And it was a good shot.

Or a lucky shot.

The slug penetrated the rear tire and flattened it instantly. The bike fishtailed. Will came down off the pegs. He had ridden enough fishtailing bikes to know it was out of control, and no amount of experience or expertise could help him to regain it.

The motorcycle careened across a narrow dirt road run-ning parallel with the ridge.

Will sucked in his breath; his eyes widened in horror as

he saw that the ground fell away sharply—too sharply for any hope of hugging the curvature. Not when he was moving at such a fast speed. He knew that the bike was a "dead horse"—a racing term used to describe broken cycles that litter a course.

And he knew he was a "dead duck."

The bike shot out over the lip of the canyon, hung suspended in mid air for a split second, then began its plunge. Will threw himself away from the bike, at enough of an angle so that despite their equal forward momentum, he would not crash into the machine further down the slope. If he got that far. . . .

Will somersaulted into the beginning of a spectacular plunge, maintaining a rolling action as he tried to protect his head from the boulders and rocks that littered the canyon slope. His brain was strangely calm as he accepted his fate.

He thought once of Tommy as he fell.

The rolling plunge didn't stop until Will and the motorcycle had reached the canyon floor.

At the top of the ridge, the Porsche skidded to a stop. Millard and Cortland piled out and ran to the edge of the slope, looking down into the deep canyon. Two trails of dust were visible—one heavy, which marked the descent of the bike, the other more powdery, marking Will's headlong fall.

Millard looked at Cortland, who was smiling smugly like himself. "Well," he said, "that's one down and one to go." Millard turned and headed for the Porsche. "And now let's finish Mr. Evel Knievel once and for all."

25

Tunnel Vision

NORMAN Clark wheeled the duplicate rig as fast as he dared along the winding road north. He was feeling reckless and he was feeling good. North meant the border. And the border meant his cut of fifty million smackeroos. He was whistling "Seventy-six Trombones" from *The Music Man*.

Barton sat beside him, occasionally glancing into the rearview mirror, and annoyed at Clark's whistling. He had always hated *The Music Man*.

"See anything?" asked Clark, when he had finished the tune.

"Relax," said Barton. "If you want, I'll take the wheel."

"I'm fine. I just wanna know what's back there."

"Empty road. Satisfied?"

"I haven't seen the Porsche for a while."

"Don't worry about the Porsche. Millard and Cortland can take care of themselves."

"Just make sure that road stays empty."

The rig squealed around one final bend before hitting a straightaway. A ridge of a hill paralleled the road along this stretch, and neither Clark nor Barton saw that Knievel was atop that ridge, moving at a steady speed that equaled the rig's.

"What's that ahead?" asked Clark nervously.

Barton checked the road map spread across the dashboard. "A tunnel. Nothing but a tunnel. Relax, Clark. Think about all the dough waiting for us on the other side."

Neither of them saw the cycle that now accelerated and shot ahead of the rig, continuing to run along the ridge above the highway.

As he approached the tunnel, Knievel curved the bike so that he was now riding atop the tunnel.

Just before the rig passed into the arched opening, Clark thought he saw a glimpse of bright orange. "You see anything back there?" he asked Barton.

Barton shrugged indifferently. "Cactus plants. Maybe a gila monster. So what?"

"Nothing. I guess I didn't see nothing."

As he rode the top of the tunnel, Knievel could sense the movement of the rig beneath him. He gauged the remaining length of the tunnel, his speed, the speed of the rig, and decided to take the risk.

He wasn't thinking of his own safety. He was thinking of some other people.

Tommy Atkins.

Kate Morgan.

Trapped in the rear of the van, destined to be silenced before the rig crossed the border and was stopped by Customs. They knew too much—and Knievel had already seen the lengths to which Millard and Cortland would go to ensure the safe arrival of the multimillion-dollar drug shipment. He was certain now that Millard had been responsible for the death of Ben Andrews and Jessie.

And Knievel knew what he had to do.

Ironic, he thought, that he was about to make his most spectacular jump and there wasn't a single spectator to see it.

At the last moment he realized that he was moving too fast and he throttled down.

And then he flew off the lip of the tunnel into space. There was nothing beneath him.

Had he miscalculated? If so, the fall to the highway was certain to kill him. Both tires would blow under the impact and he would be thrown headlong into the air. He tried not to think of how he might look afterwards, moving at that speed. After scraping across the concrete highway.

They would be scooping him up into gunny sacks.

But then the cab of the trailer was beneath him . . . then the long, flat surface of the roof of the van. Plenty of room for a landing.

He arced downward gracefully, completely cutting his power, and ready to hit the brake the instant he touched down.

The bike landed squarely in the center of the roof. It would have continued forward, probably dropping off the side of the van under its own forward momentum, except that Knievel had hit the brake at the proper moment and had thrown his weight to the left, forcing the bike over on its side.

That had stopped the bike, but not Knievel.

He skidded across the roof, coming to rest with his buttocks hanging over the edge of the trailer and his fingers clawing desperately for something to grasp. He rolled away from the edge and let out a loud sigh.

It had been close, but he had only minor scratches. This was one stunt Knievel prayed he would never be asked to duplicate.

In the cab, Clark and Barton had both heard the loud thump of Knievel's fall, and both had sat in silence, each afraid to ask what could have created such a distinctive, out-of-place sound.

"What was that?" Clark finally asked.

"How the hell do I know," barked Barton. He was no longer Mr. Cool. That sound had been a warning.

Trouble. And they both knew it.

"I'd better pull over," said Clark.

Barton disagreed. "Keep this rig moving. Millard said not to stop for anything. You just keep your head. I'm gonna go up topside and take a look around. I just wanna make sure we don't have any unwanted guests."

In the trailer, the sound of Knievel's landing was even more ominous to Kate and Tommy. They clung to each other, staring up at the ceiling and continuing to avoid falling tools as the rig once again began to take sharp curves at high speed.

"I swear," said Kate, "I think someone is walking around up there."

At that moment Barton was pulling himself out of the truck's cab onto the top of the rig. In his right hand was a .45 automatic, a souvenir of his World War II experiences. The coupling mechanism that held the cab and trailer together served as a trestle for Barton.

He worked his way to the mooring, then glanced around to the side of the rig. He saw a ladder that led to the roof. He began to inch his way along the side of the trailer toward the ladder.

On the roof, Knievel was flat on his belly, moving toward a ladder on the driver's side of the trailer. Once he reached that ladder, he would have no trouble reaching the coupling mechanism, and in turn the cab.

Knievel had just descended the ladder as Barton pulled himself onto the roof of the trailer. He hurried to Knievel's overturned motorcycle.

So . . . he'd seen something atop the tunnel after all. That crazy Knievel must have tried to land the bike when they came out of the tunnel. Only he didn't land right and got thrown off. Right now he was probably undergoing a mating ritual with a Pitahaya cactus bush.

So much for Evel Knievel.

Barton turned and started back down the ladder.

As Barton worked his way downward, a rung at a time, Knievel was reaching the coupling mechanism and moving toward the driver's door of the cab.

If Clark had glanced into his rear-view mirror at the right moment, he would have seen a mass of orange, topped by a mean face, coming at him.

Instead, his eyes were welded to the highway, for the road continued to twist and turn through deep gorges. Even when Knievel reached the cab door and began to push down on the handle, Clark was still unaware of his danger.

It was only when the door flipped open and he felt a rush of warm air that Clark saw Knievel.

It was the second time that day, in the presence of Evel Knievel, that he had been too late.

Clark turned his face in surprise, just in time to bring his jaw in line with Knievel's fist. The blow threw him across the seat, his arms becoming entangled in the road map stretched across the dashboard. Clark tried to throw the map at Knievel, but the wind picked it up and sucked it through the partly open door.

There were lug wrenches and other tools on the floor of the cab and Clark groped blindly for one of them. His fingers closed around a Crescent just as Knievel slid into the driver's seat, trying to control the steering wheel with one hand while he shook Clark with the other.

Clark brought up the wrench, lashing at Knievel. The swing was close, brushing Knievel's face. The wrench plunged downward against his thighs, making painful but not damaging contact.

Knievel dared to remove his other hand from the wheel long enough to deliver a flurry of punches to Clark's face. Clark groaned, dropped the Crescent, and slumped against the passenger door, unconscious.

Knievel swung around just in time to swerve the rig and avoid crashing into a farmer's pick-up filled with crates of chickens. When the road ahead was clear again. Knievel slammed on the air brakes.

In the same instant he twisted the wheel hard right.

Atop the rig, Barton never knew what happened. One moment he was getting ready to climb back into the rig, the next he was hurtling through space.

He saw the Pitahaya cactus coming up to greet him and threw his arms in front of his face.

It didn't offer much resistance.

He crashed against the cactus, sheering off its top as he rolled down the embankment, coming to rest and never moving again. The .45 automatic had fallen from his hand and rested ten feet from his outstretched, broken body.

Knievel's twisting of the wheel had served a dual purpose. It eliminated Barton as a possible threat, and it jackknifed the trailer so that it slid into a drainage ditch and slammed against the overhanging bank. The rear of the rig remained thrust out across the highway, and would block traffic from both directions.

Kate picked up a wrench from the littered floor of the workshop and stood near the door as it creaked open and a shaft of sunlight fell across Tommy's face.

She was all ready to swing at the head that poked through the opening when Tommy cried, "Evel!"

The wrench fell to the floor with a heavy thud.

"Hey," said Knievel, as if his feelings were hurt.

"Evel," said Kate with a sense of great relief. She fell into his arms.

"I thought you crashed," said Tommy, clutching Knievel's leg. "What happened?"

"Don't worry about me, little guy. How you doing? You okay?"

Kate began sniffling. "I . . . I hate criers," she said, wiping the tears from her eyes.

"It's only human, *Mzzz*," said Knievel in a lighthearted fashion.

"Did you get my dad out of the sanitarium?"

Knievel released Kate, turning to face Tommy. "Sure I did. He played the decoy. Got that Porsche away so I could come down to help you."

Tommy was almost afraid to ask. "Is he all right?"

175

"I think he's all right, pardner. We'll have to wait a while to find out."

Tommy frowned, clearly worried.

Knievel picked up a coil of rope from the floor of the van. "Don't worry, Tommy, your dad'll be okay. He knows how to handle a bike better'n me. Kate, you stay here. Tommy, I need a hand from you. I got one of those goons down and I want to make sure he stays down. Come on with me for a minute."

It took Knievel, with Tommy's assistance, only a few minutes to bind Clark with the rope and load him into the rear of the van, securing the door with a sense of satisfaction.

All the while, Tommy was looking up and down the highway for some sign of his father.

Knievel saw his anxiety and patted him on the back. "Now look, Tommy, don't worry. I'm gonna take care of your dad. But I don't want you to wait here. That Porsche could come back at any time. I want you both to wait behind those rocks over there until I get back. You don't come out for anyone. Understand?"

Kate and Tommy nodded, took positions behind the indicated rocks several hundred yards back from the main highway, and watched as Knievel took one of the bikes from the rear of the van.

In less than a minute he wasn't even a speck on the highway.

26

Ride to Death

BOTH Millard and Knievel were pushing their machines so hard that they at first passed each other as blurred objects—Knievel moving south, Millard racing north.

Millard, suddenly realizing who was on the bike, threw the Porsche into another skillful slide and in moments was charging after the skedaddling Harley.

Knievel took the first dirt road leading off the main highway, where a sign indicated VERDE only two kilometers away.

Verde was a sleepy Mexican village in the middle of its traditional midafternoon siesta as Knievel rolled through the center of town, the Porsche close on his tail.

Knievel turned into a narrow side street and cursed when he saw an ancient cart blocking the path. Its equally ancient owner suddenly displayed tendencies toward youth when he saw that the madman behind the handlebars had no intention of stopping. The old man threw himself headfirst through the window of an adobe hut; fortunately, it was without glass.

Knievel "blipped" his throttle in quick, short bursts, clearing the carburetor of excess gas. For he knew that throttle control would be vital if he were going to "walk over the obstacle."

He simultaneously "blipped" the throttle and pulled the front wheel off the ground—a "lofting" maneuver which enabled him to climb right over the sloped side of the wagon, overturning it as he came down.

The Porsche pulled up behind the wagon; Millard saw there was no way he could pass and he shot backwards in reverse, killing three roosters too slow to get out of the way.

Cantina del Agua Caliente was usually a relaxed establishment, where the weary and thirsty citizens of Verde

177

gathered to drink tequila, *mezcal* and *aguaridinete* and exchange stories about the heat or of the afternoon's work or of the *bonita señoritas* who could be seen passing through the village on their way to the nearby river for water.

Cantina del Agua Caliente was now the scene of havoc.

Knievel's motorcycle crashed through the swinging doors, which were no longer swinging doors but *sailing* doors.

He gunned his way into the cantina tables, sending most of the patrons running for their lives, praying that God was still with them.

Knievel plucked a bottle of tequila from one of the few tables he had yet to overturn, took a healthy drink and returned the bottle to its owner. *"Gracias, amigo."*

"Por nada," said the peasant.

The Porsche had just pulled up to the steps of the cantina when Knievel came flying through the nonexistent swinging doors. Millard and Cortland ducked as the front wheel of the motorcycle passed inches above their heads. The bike just barely cleared the rear of the Porsche, kicking up a spurt of dust that had Cortland coughing for the next minute. Millard cursed the bravura of his adversary and turned the Porsche about. "We're gonna get that sonofabitch, so help me," he vowed.

"If he doesn't get us first," corrected Cortland, who was wiping the dust from his face with a grimy handkerchief.

"No way," promised Millard, following after Knievel's dust. Cortland stood in the seat, hoping for the kind of expert (or was it lucky?) shot that had brought down Will Atkins.

Cortland glanced at Millard and almost felt like saying it was time to give this madness up, that they were risking more than just the drug shipment. They were now putting their lives on the line in this insane chase across the desert of Mexico.

But Cortland saw the determination in Millard's face and knew there was no way he could convince him to give up pursuit. And if they could get rid of Knievel, and move the duplicate rig across the border, they would be rich for life. He could quit his practice, the Organization, everything. Just live in luxury on the Riviera, jet-hopping from capital to capital, surrounding himself with beautiful women. The temptations of such a life were too alluring, he decided.

Knievel cut through an alleyway (two *bonita señoritas* with water ewers on their heads leaped out of the way, but still managed not to spill a drop of their precious load) and crashed stoically through a plank fence to emerge in a horse corral.

A palomino reared up, as if to paw Knievel with its forelegs and knock him from the bike, but he swerved and performed a wheelie around the corral, spooking the animals and forcing them to run wildly 'n circles.

Into the thunderous roar of hoofbeats and swirling dust came the Porsche in its own fashion—by taking the main gate head-on. The front end of the Targa was like a battering ram, splintering wood as it charged into the corral.

Knievel hunched over on his Harley, concealed behind the milling, pawing horses. Sneakily he worked his way toward the half-destroyed gate.

Too late, Millard saw what Knievel was up to and he spun the wheel, sending the Porsche into a skid that was aided greatly by the fresh piles of horse manure scattered under the tires.

Knievel zoomed through the broken boards, the Porsche directly behind him, as if pulled by some magnetic force emanating from the bike. The daredevil angled his cycle into another alleyway, then realized belatedly that he had made a wrong turn.

Dead end.

Built into the far wall, however, was a window that began almost at ground level. Knievel revved the bike and aimed for the opening, gritting his teeth. Fortunately, there was no glass, only an old Venetian blind that easily gave way before the nose of the Harley.

As the covering fell away, Knievel found himself atop the bar of the Cantina del Agua Caliente, which the bartender was in the process of wiping clean. He caroomed along the bar, passing the barkeep, who was frozen in dismay, and sending at least a dozen tequila glasses into shattered oblivion.

There was a plate-glass window at the end of the bar counter which Knievel passed right on through. The word "AGUA" disintegrated before the Harley and Knievel came down on the sidewalk, overturning a pickle barrel, flattening a discarded sombrero and knocking loose one of the two-by-fours that kept the saloon on an even keel.

The Porsche emerged from the side of the saloon just as Knievel headed back toward the main highway. Cortland snapped off another hopeless shot, saw that he had missed by several yards when the bullet chipped the ear of a yucca plant, and angrily fell back into the seat to insert a new seven-shot clip into the Sterling.

Outside Verde, halfway between the town and the main highway, was the old Verde Quarry, which in more prosperous days had been the center of much activity and had helped put Verde on the map.

The quarry, which had been deserted for years, was reached by several dirt roads (now overgrown with weeds and bushes and frequently invaded by tumbleweeds) which eventually dropped off sharply into a yawning pit.

Knievel was now streaking up one of those roads, Cortland and Millard hot behind. Suddenly Knievel saw that the road ahead seemed to end abruptly at a kind of precipice: what lay beyond?

For an instant he thought he'd swerve off, but then he realized that the Porsche, so eagerly dogging his trail, would be headed for the same disaster—if indeed disaster waited at the end of the road.

There was a chance . . . perhaps his only chance . . .

Knievel decided to accelerate even faster.

So did the Porsche.

Exactly as he had hoped.

There was no compassion in Knievel now. Not when the possibility existed that Millard and Cortland had finished off Will, and were going to finish him off next.

And then Kate and Tommy.

Coldly, calculatingly, Knievel judged the distance to the edge of the quarry, gauged his speed, and said some words that passed his lips only on extra-special occasions: a prayer.

Knievel's bike streaked unhesitatingly toward the lip of the plateau. It was as he had anticipated.

Drop-off! Sheer and deadly.

Knievel initiated the most crucial skid of his life as a motorcyclist and daredevil extraordinaire. If he did not begin the slide soon enough he would certainly plunge over the edge—and the fall was too great to expect any chance of survival. If he began the slide too soon, and Millard saw him swerving, it would give him enough time to bring the Porsche to a safe stop.

His timing had to be perfect.

He gave the Harley one last burst of acceleration and leaned hard to his left, standing on the pegs.

At first he thought he had waited too long. The edge of the

tire was hugging the last few inches of the precipice—if the angle of his turn went any farther he would go over the edge.

But he had calculated well—exactly to the inch.

And the bike continued along the lip of the plateau, no longer threatened.

The Porsche wasn't so lucky.

In his fury to get Knievel, a blind fury that had destroyed his caution and his concern for his own safety, Millard had barreled toward the quarry at top speed.

When he finally saw the gaping pit it was too late.

And even though he turned the wheel adeptly, hitting the brakes to purposely fishtail the car, there wasn't the room needed to successfully complete the turn in time.

The Porsche was sideways to the drop-off, almost coming to a stop, when the front right tire no longer had anything to grip. Then the back right tire had nothing to grip.

And then the Porsche was yawling to the right, flipping over so Millard and Cortland could see the fate that awaited them below.

And then the Porsche was falling.

Cortland screamed. He turned to give Millard one final accusing look. But Millard was frozen with fear, his hands still gripping the wheel, his eyes on the ground that was coming up so swiftly, and so friendlessly, to welcome them.

Millard opened his mouth to scream just as the Porsche struck ground and exploded.

From the rim of the plateau, Knievel watched the burning Porsche. He could feel no emotion for the two men burning to death inside.

He shut their screams out of his mind and pointed the Harley back toward the main highway, his thoughts now on Kate and Tommy.

And the fate of Will Atkins.

27

Reunion

THEY waited behind the rocks as Knievel had instructed them, but they did not wait patiently.

Patience had evaporated under the hot afternoon sun for Kate and Tommy. The boy paced desperately from medium-sized boulder to tiny-sized boulder and back again.

"Why don't they come?" he asked for the tenth time.

"They will," Kate tried to reassure Tommy. "Evel will come."

Tommy turned away from the sun, wiping the sweat from his forehead. Kate did likewise, realizing that they couldn't stay under this blistering sun much longer without protection.

Suddenly Tommy pointed excitedly. "Look, over there."

Kate squinted against the whitish glare. "I don't see anything, Tommy."

"I do," he insisted. "Something moved out there."

Kate was full of sympathy when she replied, "Tommy, it's your imagination."

But Tommy wasn't to be swayed. "It always was before. But not this time." He broke away from Kate, running toward the hillside where he thought he had seen movement.

"Tommy," cried Kate, "come back here."

"Dad!" cried Tommy. "Dad!"

Kate's face was flushed with excitement. Now she too saw something moving among the rocks—still too far away to identify. Evel had told them not to move for anyone. And now someone was coming—but who? She started after Tommy, praying it was neither Millard nor Cortland.

Her fears were unfounded. It was Will Atkins who came stumbling down out of the rocks, his clothing torn, his face and arms covered with lacerations, bruises and scrapes.

Tommy ran into his arms and Will swooped up the boy.

"Dad, oh, Dad." Tommy was too overcome with emotion to speak again for a while.

"Tommy, Tommy," Will repeated over and over, as though he had always wanted to say that name but had always been afraid to until now. "I've got you at last."

After an interminable hug, Will put Tommy down and began to explain. "I have to tell you something . . . about . . ."

"You already have," said Tommy.

Will clammed up, realizing that a lot of words weren't necessary. Explanations could come later.

Kate watched the reunion from a distance, deciding that this was too personal a moment for her to intrude.

The sound of a Harley made her jump and she whirled about, relieved to see Knievel pulling off the main highway.

The bike was battered, he was battered, but the smile on his face told her it was nothing his good humor couldn't overcome.

"Am I glad to see you," said Kate.

"Same here." Knievel climbed laboriously off the bike, banging the dust from his orange coveralls and removing his helmet. His face was heavily streaked with dirt.

Kate laughed when she saw his face; he laughed too, knowing he must look a mess. He took her in his arms and kissed her gently. She kissed him back, less gently. He stirred and felt alive again.

"What happened out there?" she asked, pulling back.

"Couple of things I had to take care of."

"Millard?"

"He and Cortland are dead. Drove themselves right off a cliff. With a little help from me. But I didn't find Will."

Kate pointed toward the hillside, where Tommy and Will were engaged in some deep discussion.

"He's okay," said Kate. "Will found us."

"Hey, they finally found each other."

"Like we did," added Kate.

Knievel nodded. He wiped some of the grime from his forehead and said tiredly, "Never thought I'd be happy to get off a bike."

"Just an ordinary day in the life of Evel Knievel. Right?"

"It has its ups and downs. Stick around and find out all about them, Kate."

"I work too, remember?"

"Okay, so you could do the story layout of my life."

"You've got years and years of living yet."

"And you can spend them with me, getting that layout."

"I'll have to take it under advisement."

"Do that," said Knievel, grinning.

28

The Jaws of Death

GOOD *afternoon, ladies and gentlemen. This is Frank Gifford once again, speaking to you from sunny Mexico, from joyous Estadia del Sol, Stadium of the Sun, where hopefully last week's disaster, in which famous bike jumper Jessie Hammond died, will turn into this week's victory.*

But it won't be easy. As though to wipe out what happened here, Evel Knievel has chosen to face a different hazard, one which makes today's jump the most dangerous of his career.

Down in the center of the arena is a water tank, which contains ten of the most ferocious man-eating sharks I've ever had the discomfort to see. There's no roof on that water tank, which means there's nothing to prevent anyone from falling in should he happen to be passing overhead. And passing overhead is exactly what the world-famous daredevil Evel Knievel will be doing this afternoon. Those sharks are king-sized, deadly and ravenous, ladies and gentlemen, and if Evel misses, he'll fall to instant, agonizing death.

The sight of those evil, bloodthirsty creatures of the deep sends a shudder through this crowd . . . any one of them could easily tear a man apart in a matter of seconds. Evel will be leaping over a dozen as he jumps toward a happy landing here in Mexico.

Tommy stood on the edge of the field beside Will and Kate. All three were watching Evel Knievel as he rode his jump bike to the turnaround room. He reappeared almost immediately, waving to the crowd.

"No delays this time," said Will.

"This time," said Tommy, "he's really gonna do it."

"You're right," agreed Kate, adjusting her Nikon and gazing into the viewfinder. "And this is one jump I want to have a picture of."

"It won't be his last," spoke up Will. "You're going to see that man jumping a lot more times before he's through."

Knievel threw one final half-wave, half-salute and the crowd cheered. And then he was zooming down the ramp, building speed to ninety-five miles an hour, and then he was past the end of the takeoff ramp, he was airborne, flying high above the ground, soaring above the swimming sharks, heading straight and true for the touch-down ramp.

Once again Knievel felt the thrust of the engine, the surge of the machine. Once again he and the machine were as one. This time it was the perfect union he sought with each jump, for it was a precision landing. And a new world's record.

And the crowd, in a rising crescendo of thunder, paid homage to the last American hero of the twentieth century:

"VIVA KNIEVEL!"
"VIVA KNIEVEL!"
"VIVA KNIEVEL!"

29

Interview

PARDON, señor, con permiso. *I would like to ask you a few of the questions.*

You a journal jock, *amigo?* Always got time to answer a few questions. What's up, *muchacho?*

There are rumors, señor, *that you might be performing some jumps for SeñorAgajanian, the famous promoter.*

Sí, sí, I ran into Aggie down here in Mexico and we discussed that possibility. Now that I'm wrapped up here south of the border I'm thinking seriously about going north to do some jumping.

There is talk that Gene Romero is now numero uno *among the jumpers of bikes.*

That's a lot of talk, *amigo,* nothing more. There's only one *numero uno.* And you're talking to him right now.

Pardon, señor, *but there is the question I must ask. Perhaps they ask it of you many times, but the curiosity in this country is* mucho grande. *Why,* señor, *do you take such great risks to make the jump?*

Same reason why a man eats his first hamburger, climbs a mountain or tries to go to the moon.

Como?

Because it's there, *amigo,* because it's there.

**ECOLOGICAL DESPERADOES WREAK HAVOC
TO RESTORE THE BEAUTY OF THE
AMERICAN LANDSCAPE**

THE MONKEY WRENCH GANG

A novel by EDWARD ABBEY

They are a madcap group, drawn together by their hatred
for the ugly symbols of technology. They wreck bridges,
demolish bulldozers, set billboards ablaze, and stay one
step ahead of the law on the path to their ultimate goal—
to blow up the Glen Canyon Dam, just north of the Grand
Canyon on the rushing Colorado River.

"It's a wildly funny, infinitely wise, near to tragic tale . . .
What a thing of beauty is Abbey's THE MONKEY
WRENCH GANG." *Houston Chronicle*

"Edward Abbey is the Thoreau of the American desert . . .
a writer one would not want to miss." *Washington Post*

"Beats hell out of BONNIE AND CLYDE or BUTCH
CASSIDY!" *Playboy*

 30114/$1.95

GANG 11-76

AVON ⬡ THE BEST IN
BESTSELLING ENTERTAINMENT!

THE ONE NOVEL YOU
WILL READ THIS YEAR AS THOUGH
YOUR LIFE DEPENDED ON IT!

THE DEADLY MESSIAH

DAVID CAMPBELL HILL / ALBERT FAY HILL

A terrible plague—deadlier than swine flu, more
mysterious than "Legionnaire's Disease"—grips the
United States. Ravaged victims claw past rotting
bodies. Eyes stare from sunken, twisted faces.
No cause, no cure is known . . .

On the trail of this unspeakable evil are Jess Barrett,
Heisman trophy winner and scientist; Micah
Maruyama, aide to the President; and Vera
Norman, beautiful, brilliant astrologer . . .

40 million will die horribly unless these three can
find and destroy the "deadly messiah!"

"AN IRRESISTIBLE PAGE-TURNER . . .
THIS ONE CANNOT BE PUT DOWN!"
Library Journal

 AVON   32466 $1.95

DEM 4-77